TORR
Castle

TORR Castle

IRENE CODDING

Pentland Press, Inc.
www.pentlandpressusa.com

PUBLISHED BY PENTLAND PRESS, INC.
5122 Bur Oak Circle, Raleigh, North Carolina 27612
United States of America
919-782-0281

ISBN 1-57197-275-7
Library of Congress Control Number: 2001 131147

Copyright © 2001 Irene Codding
All rights reserved, which includes the right to reproduce
this book or portions thereof in any form whatsoever
except as provided by the U.S. Copyright Law.

Printed in the United States of America

Note to reader:

Regarding Torr Castle, it does exist under another name in southern England. The local saying there is, "When one can see the castle it is going to rain. When one can't see the castle it is raining."

Some of the events in this novel are based upon historical facts. Some events are fiction. The true events are often much more strange than the fiction.

I have attempted to give a hint of the style and manner of the language which was used at this time. Spellings are often those used in Old English.

Irene Codding

The remains of Torr Castle still stand gaunt and stark upon their steep hill unto this day. The roofs have all gone, and the walls damaged by nature and by humans. None take shelter there now. The only inhabitants are the rooks that fly above in endless dark spirals, crying the dirge of the castle.

CHAPTER 1

Evening of December 24 in the year A.D. 950 brought a darkening of a sky already gray with clouds. The wind freshened, bringing stinging needles of sleet to pelt Padraik the minnesinger and his donkey as they entered the village on their way to Torr Castle. The small hooves of the donkey slipped and slid as he crossed the slates of the bridge to the castle gate. Padraik rang the iron bell attached to the gatehouse door. When a face appeared at the peephole, Padraik shouted, "I bring a message to King Ethelred from Alfred, king of Sussex."

"Slide it through the arrowslit; the king will get it."

"No. My commission is to deliver this parchment in person. That I must do, at peril of my life."

"How do I know you are no robber, set upon taking life and possessions?"

"Let me in, and I will prove honesty."

The small door in the large castle gate was opened cautiously. Padraik and his donkey were glad to step in the sheltering archway of the gate, where the sleet did not reach. Padraik drew from under his cloak a parchment roll sealed with the royal seal of Sussex. This seal the gatekeeper had seen before on communications from the king of Sussex to his daughter Margrethe, wife of Ethelred, king of Wessex. "Looks right enough," said the gatekeeper. "But why could you not arrive whilst yet it was day?"

"Small John, my steed here, has small legs," replied Padraik, patting the donkey lovingly. "And small hooves as well, which made many a slip on the icy road coming up through the hills."

"Wait you here, while I fetch a guide and a carrying lanthorne. Much bother on such a night." The gatekeeper grumbled away into the gatehouse, from which there soon came loud shouting and a thud. He came back with a reluctant lout of a lad whose sullen face bore the mark of a recent blow. "The boy here will guide you, first to the stables for the beast, then to the king's hall."

Managing to hold his lanthorne in such a way as to shed as much shadow as light on the path, the lad walked slowly across the broad, open tournament yard, then up a steep slope to the first of the stone castle buildings. These were the stables, well set of gray stone, better than many houses in the village.

Small John shied back from the odor that came from the door of the stable. He entered timidly and found the warmth comforting. He humphed a few times to let it be known that he was accustomed to cleaner stables, then began nibbling the dirty hay in the stone manger.

Padraik removed a long wooden case from the pack that Small John had been carrying. Taking the case with him he followed the boy to the castle.

The boy beat on the outer castle door. The guardsman took time in answering. He beat on the door again, and yet again, before there was a response.

The guardsman came to the door, wiping the grease from his mouth with an already greasy sleeve. He belched loudly, and said, "Who be it, why be it, and how be it?"

"Padraik, minnesinger to the king of Sussex, bearing a commission to be given into the hand of the king of Wessex. That answers your first two questions. How be it is near frozen. For the love of our sweet Lord, open up!"

"Give me the message, and I will take it to the king."

"That I cannot do. I am sworn to deliver it myself." The guardsman opened the door. Padraik turned and flipped a small coin to the lad with the lanthorne. The boy seemed nearly too surprised to pick it up. He tucked the coin quickly into his garments and vanished into the night.

Following the guardsman into the great hall of the castle, Padraik saw that the trestle table was still in use. The evening meal had lasted long, and most of the diners were now occupied in cracking nuts and sipping wine.

King Ethelred sat in the high seat, and beside him was a red-cheeked, slovenly dame well advanced in pregnancy. Padraik's eyes searched in vain for the queen, Margrethe, who had always been a favorite of his when she was a girl in her father's household.

"I bear a commission to the king and to the queen," said Padraik.

"Speak on, we are here," demanded Ethelred.

"I see a king, but not a queen."

"Blind you are then, my queen sits beside me."

"No, Sire, that is not the daughter of my master, King Alfred. I doubt not that this lady stands in need of husband, but you are not he. Where sits your queen?

In reply, the king pointed to the far end of the table. In the gloom at the end of the room Padraik had not recognized a thin, pale woman with red-rimmed eyes as the former princess Margrethe. Padraik went to kneel before her. "My lady queen."

She looked surprised. "That sounds like Padraik's voice. Is it Padraik? Truly Padraik?"

Her white face flushed with pleasure when he said, "Yes, truly Padraik, my Lady."

"Come up, come up," said the king motioning to them. Margrethe stood up, looking confused until a plain-looking knight took her hand courteously. He lead her gently to the king, moving slowly as she trod uncertainly.

The king whispered to Helene, who demurred, then vacated her chair with ill grace. As Helene passed the knight and Margrethe she said tauntingly, "Behold, a queen as blind and unlovely as a white mole."

Margrethe, startled by her venom, kept her regal manner. "Even blinded eyes can see the jewels of a queen being disported by a strumpet." Margrethe smiled determinedly as she took her rightful place beside the king.

Padraik took the sealed scroll from his inner cloak and presented it to the king.

King Ethelred clapped his hands, calling, "Cleric, cleric, where is the cleric?" A small gray man in a gray robe hastened to him. "Here, read me this," commanded Ethelred.

"My Lord, you know I do not read the English, I read but Latin, as does any true scholar."

"Rest easy then, cleric," said Padraik. "This is the purest of Latin."

"So say you."

"So say I, who wrote it."

The cleric broke the seal, and studied the message.

"Well?" demanded the king.

"Poorly written, poorly written. Who can decipher such a podge of crow tracks?"

"I can," said Padraik, taking the scroll. "Have I permission to read it out?"

The king signaled assent.

Padraik read:

> To Ethelred, King of Wessex, and to my daughter Margrethe, Queen of Wessex, and their court; know that we shall be with you in three days. Our cortege will require hospitality for ourselves, 40 knights at arms, 20 bowmen, equerries, grooms, and horses. We would remind our royal children that the time has come for the fosterage of their son, Edward. He shall return with us to our court when we depart. We send this by the hand Padraik, master minnesinger, that he may refresh your court with new music. May the grace of our Lord and His peace be you at this season of the Holy Nativity.
>
> *Alfred Rex.*
> *His seal*

Margrethe clasped her hands joyfully, "My father and his court coming here. That is good news. Where is our son?"

"Where he is every night at this time," replied the king. "Under the table, asleep. The child has no stomach for wine at all, and him near seven years old."

Padraik looked under the trestle table. There lay little prince Edward, face flushed scarlet, deep in sodden sleep near the feet of the king.

"Majesty, should he not be a-bed?"

"He does well where he is. The rushes are as soft as his bed. When we are ready to retire, the boy will be bedded. Not before."

Margrethe asked, "Padraik, do you have your lute with you?"

"Of course, good lady, is music your desire?"

"If it please his Majesty," said Margrethe.

His majesty was busily cracking walnuts on the table by pounding them with the haft of his bodkin. He signaled the steward for more wine and drained his refilled cup before replying, "Music can wait until we have eat." He gestured to Padraik, "Go find a seat down there. Have a bowl of wine."

Padraik bowed and went to locate a place for himself. A bowl of wine and a hard manchet of bread were brought to him. Padraik had not thought himself hungry until he began to eat. Then it was difficult to restrain himself politely. He tore the bread into sops to dip in the wine bowl and found it very refreshing. The great hall, which had seemed cool before now felt warm, so that Padraik loosened the strings at the neck of his tunic.

The king had finally had his fill of the nuts, and he summoned the servants to remove the trestle table. The still-sleeping prince was lifted onto the chair with his mother.

Padraik removed his lute from its wooden case and examined it carefully. No dampness seemed to have reached it. He tightened the strings, tuning and turning until the exact pitch for each was reached. When the king indicated that he was ready to listen, Padraik went to stand before the royal couple. He bowed to them and to the assemblage and said, "This tune is new come from France. A song for the nativity." In a tenor voice, with a sweet lilt to it he began.

> *The virgin hat borne a flower this night*
> *It is our Savior, sweet delight,*
> *Ha-ah-la-la-la, Angels do sing*
> *Ha-ah-la-la-la, Rejoice for the King.*
> *The news it pleased not Herod the King*
> *He hated the song the Angels did sing*
> *Ha-ah-la-la-la his anger was wild*
> *Ha-ah-la-la-la decreed death for the Child.*
> *The angels unto good Joseph and Mary*
> *Warning of Herod's plot did carry*
> *Ha-ah-la-la-la, they hasted away*
> *Ha-ah-la-la-la, to Egypt's safety.*

The melody was repeated by the lute, ending in a minor chord. Polite applause came, stopping abruptly when it was noticed that the king did not applaud. Margrethe looked much restored by the music. She said, "Oh, Padraik, can you play for me the song I used to like so much, the one about the lark in spring, which did both fly and sing?"

"My lady means the song 'The Birdes of May.' Certainly I will sing it for you."

"No," said the king. "No. We like not such stuff. Give us a good lusty ballad. What about 'The Miller's Wife'?"

Much against his own desires, Padraik struck the three strong chords that prefaced the song.

> *The millers wife is broad in the beam*
> *Round and round the miller grinds corn.*
> *When pinched in the butte she loudly does scream*
> *Round and round the miller grinds corn.*

The assemblage stamped and clapped in time to this music, taking their lead from the king. Seventeen verses followed, each more bawdy than the one before. By the end Padraik was heartily wishing the song to hell.

Padraik now pleaded weariness and asked leave to retire. The young prince stirred restlessly, and Margrethe desired to take him to his bed. The king gave his consent. Padraik put his lute carefully back into its case and followed Margrethe, as the gentle knight who had lead her earlier now hoisted the sleeping boy in his arms and carried him from the room. He walked slowly, so that Margrethe could cling to his tunic for guidance.

On the steep stone stairway leading to the upper chambers Margrethe moved confidently. Her feet had learned the position and condition of each step, and she knew which stones had worn and chipped. There was never a banister on stairs like these, and they were so narrow that two people could pass one another only at the peril of the one on the outside.

"Have a care, Padraik," Margrethe called. "This stair is where my sweet gentlewoman Berta fell to her death. She was wife to Karyl, the good knight who leads us."

"Lord have mercy on her soul," Padraik crossed himself.

"Indeed. Her death left me with only three ladies in waiting. Then old Anna was found dead in her bed. She was old, past fifty years. That left me with two ladies. Alicia died for the reason that she worked with me on the new tapestry, which now hangs in the great hall. A poisonous dye had been used on the yellow thread. Helene did no stitching with the yellow, she was ill of a phlegm. We were using so little yellow in the pattern that Alicia and I could complete the tapestry in a short time. But my eyes became so tired. I rubbed them and rubbed them, and rubbed the poison from the thread into them. I was unable to see, and sick as well from the poison, although we didn't know the source then. Faithful Alicia decided to complete the tapestry alone, which she did. Then she fell raving sick, her hair all came out, and she died. That left me with one lady, Helene, who has proved to be no lady at all. You saw her tonight with the king, sitting in my place and wearing my jewels."

"Why did you not send word to your father?"

"I did. Several letters were sent, written for me by the cleric. There was no reply."

"My lady, no such letters came to the court in Sussex."

Margrethe stopped abruptly at the top of the stairs, saying, "Edward's room is there, the first door. The room next is empty now. Why not sleep there, Padraik? My own chamber is down at the end of this hall."

"Do you manage alone now, my lady?"

"Yes, I can see for a short distance, not as far as an arm's length away. Surrounded by my own belongings, and in my own rooms I do well. I give you both a good night."

Karyl took a candle from Edward's room and lit it from the torch in the hall. Padraik looked inside the second room and found a shelf near the door with a half-burned candle on it. He lit it at the torch in the hall, then examined the room. Just a small square of gray stone, not more than three ells long, on each side and two and a half ells high. The small window had been tightly shuttered against the night air. The bed was but a bench of stone with a straw palliase covered with one thin blanket. Except for the shelf for the candle, there were no other furnishings. Padraik set his lute case on the floor and returned to the hallway. Margrethe had shut the door to her chamber. The door to Edward's room was still open. Padraik looked in. Karyl was gently removing Edward's shoes. He untied his leggings and shucked them off, then pulled a coarse blanket over the sleeping child. Motioning Padraik to keep quiet, Karyl blew out the candle, and went out, closing the door behind him. He went into Padraik's room with Padraik, and almost closed the door, leaving a crack to view the hallway.

"I fear for the life of the queen and the child," he said. "I'm glad that you have come. Perhaps with two of us who care, we can keep her safe, at least until her father arrives."

"I'm thinking that my coming may have increased the danger. If there is a conspiracy against them it will develop to a climax before King Alfred arrives."

"That could well be true. We'll have to be vigilant," replied Karyl, "I must return to the great hall now."

"Where will you be sleeping?"

"On the other side of the castle, near the king's chamber. Here, lend me your bodkin, and I'll show you how to fit that candle into the socket in this shelf."

Padraik felt his belt in amazement. His bodkin was gone. "It's been taken," he said, feeling foolish.

"Was it special in any way?"

"It had a silver haft, and the royal ensign. It was a gift to me from King Alfred himself."

"So the thief did not take it to use for himself. He took it to discredit you in some way. Try to think who could have brushed near you or crowded up close enough to take it unnoticed."

"Several came near me, but only one for very long. That one was a sturdy lad with hair like Helene's."

"That would be her younger brother, Tom. We've often suspected him of thieving like a magpie. Now I must go." Karyl hastened out and rapidly descended the long stairway.

Without his only weapon Padraik felt defenseless, until he recalled King Alfred's statement that no man is truly defenseless as long as he has the weapon of his mind.

The bodkin had most likely not been stolen to use against Margrethe. All who knew Padraik knew that he adored her and had done so from her birth. No, the harm must be intended toward the little prince. If on the morrow the prince were found stabbed to death by the weapon of the person who had slept in the room next door, who would believe that person to be innocent? And further, such a happening would discredit Padraik in everyone's eyes. When the king of Sussex and his retinue arrived, no one would listen to or believe Padraik if he carried tales of the danger and dishonor suffered by Margrethe. It seemed to Padraik that now the very walls breathed danger.

He looked out the door, saw no one, rushed into the next room, and carried out the sleeping prince, leaving his blanket behind. The prince began to snore slightly as Padraik put him in his bed, and covered him with the thin blanket. Now, how to make a dummy to take Edward's place? Perhaps use his lute case? Removing the lute and standing it carefully in a corner, Padraik took the lute to the prince's room. Placed in the prince's bed, with the rounded bottomside uppermost, and the coarse blanket folded and rumpled over it, it did have the shape of a child sleeping face down. Padraik tucked the boy's shoes and leggings in on the flat end of the case, to make a head-sized lump. Not the best of dummies, but in the half-light coming through the doorway from the hall torch it looked good enough.

Back in his own room Padraik removed his leather belt and, using it as a wedge, jammed the door shut. No one could enter quietly or easily. It would require great force to push the door inward.

Tired unto death, Padraik removed his shoes, shoved the sleeping prince back against the wall, and lay down, pulling his cloak over him as a covering. It had been a long hard day, a day that had required the utmost from Padraik since dawn. Despite his concerns, Padraik was instantly asleep.

Down in the great hall the king and his court were still carousing. Helene saw her brother beckoning to her. She left the king's side to follow Tom into an antechamber.

"Look what I have, that minnesinger's bodkin!"

"It is handsome, but how does that profit us?"

"It will be found tomorrow morn in the heart of our little prince," Tom smiled grimly.

"Must he die? What harm does he to us?"

"Use your head, sister. Would you rather the child you carry be born the heir to the throne, or that he be but the half-brother to the royal prince? As for myself, I would much prefer some day to be uncle to a king."

"I see that you are right, yet does the deed sicken me. After all, the child will soon be gone to his fosterage in Sussex."

"All the more reason to strike now. He would be a far target to hit in Sussex."

"Then do as you will, brother. Tell me no more about it. Sorry I am to know this much now." Helene walked unsteadily back to sit beside the drunken king.

He looked at her through narrowed eyes and said, "Why did you leave us without asking our permission?"

Helene smiled as lovingly as possible, placed her hand gently on her belly, and said, "Sorry, majesty, but your son grows so lusty and kicks so hard that the only way to quiet him is to walk about."

The king placed his hand near hers, and the infant delivered a mighty thump, causing the king to laugh. "Kicks like a mule, he does. We forgive you, sweeting. You're making us a strong son."

Helene's eyes filled with tears. "Yes, Lord, but he will be at best a bastard. I am not yet your wife."

"Ours you are, and ours he is. You need not mind us of promises made. They will be kept." The king drained the wine from his cup. "Time to retire now. Cover the fire, and let's away."

The assemblage made a great noisy clatter of moving chairs and stools and settles back against the walls, gathering up loose personal items, and moving to the staircases to take them to the king's tower, the queen's tower, or the servants' stalls. All wearily besotted and ready for their beds, their thoughts were fixed only on resting. All except one, who would mischief make. For so did he call murder.

A muffled and cloaked figure slipped unnoticed up the stairs to the queen's tower. At the top of the stairs it opened the first door. The dim light from the hall torch showed the shape of a child sleeping under the blanket. The figure struck downward once with a knife, which stuck in its target. No sound came. The cloaked figure exited, closing the door behind.

✟ ✟ ✟

Morning light had but grayed the darkness of the room when a small voice said, "Who are you, and why are you in my bed?"

Padraik awoke to find the child sitting up, staring at him with puzzled blue eyes. "Pardon, my prince," said Padraik. "But it is you who are in my bed."

"I don't remember you, nor how I came here."

"No. You were asleep. You were already asleep when I arrived last night before the supper was over. I am a minnesinger at the court of your grandfather. The king, your grandfather, and his court are coming here in two more days, to take you with them for your fosterage. You have been told that you will go to the court of your mother's father?"

The boy nodded. "Is that your lute? Can I play it?"

"Yes, it is mine. Sometime you can play it, but not now. Now I want you to be very quiet. We will be playing a game. Do you like games? Sure you do. We're going to give whoever comes to wake you a fright. Who comes for you in the morning?"

"The cleric. He is supposed to be my tutor, but he only teaches me to serve at mass."

"Well, then, we'll give the cleric a fright. When he comes to wake you, you won't be there. Instead, there is a dummy in your bed. When the cleric calls and you do not answer, he'll think you are dead. Isn't that a good joke?"

The child giggled, "Yes, yes. I don't like the cleric anyway. I have to call him Father John, but he wants me to do so many dumb things I think him Father Stupid."

"Shhh. Quiet now, I hear someone."

A rap on the next door. "Awake, awake my son, it is cockcrow. Time we prepare for Christ's mass." A stronger rap now. "Edward, Edward, be not such a slug-a-bed. Up now." The sounds came of the door opening, followed by a muffled gasp. "Lord have mercy on us all, the prince is dead!" The cleric went wailing down the staircase, "He is dead. The prince is dead, murdered. Murder. Murder! Our prince is killed."

Young Edward went into spasms of laughter upon hearing all this. Padraik rushed into the boy's room to remove the dummy from the bed. As he had expected, his bodkin with the silver haft was embedded well into the lute case. Padraik tossed the leggings and shoes to the prince, who began to put them on. The lute was replaced in its case, which was now no longer watertight due to the slit in its bottom. Padraik placed the bodkin in his belt, and he and the prince began to walk sedately down the stairs. From far below they could hear the echoing voices. "The prince is dead, the prince is dead."

CHAPTER 2

Padraik walked into the great hall to be greeted by an uproar. Someone shouted to him, "Heard you not? The prince is dead!"

At this, laughing merrily, Edward stepped out from behind Padraik. "No, I'm not dead! 'Twas but a bit of fun with Father John." His face sparkled with delight as he lead Padraik to table. Edward pounded on the table in good mimicry of the king, "Bread and beer, and quickly!"

Padraik protested, "My prince, fun is fun, but this is a holy day. We should go fasting to mass first, and then we can enjoy the day."

The joy went out of the child's face. He drooped, but got up from his chair as Karyl came up to them. Karyl spoke to Padraik, "The word was brought that the prince was dead. I thought it to be true. What happened?"

Padraik shook his head to indicate it best not to discuss the matter now.

Edward said, "It was a jest only. Father John is always telling me 'be peaceful, be calm' and now he's running about the castle squawking like a hen."

"The man is greatly concerned, and is even now preparing the chapel to receive your body. We had best go relieve his distress," Karyl admonished.

As the three walked to the chapel the hubbub ceased, only to begin again as soon as they had past.

Edward entered the chapel first. At the sight of him Father John fell to his knees and, crossing himself, began to pray loudly, "Lord Jesu, protect us."

Edward laughed. "I am not dead, so stop making a fuss. Let's hurry up the mass. I'm hungry."

Padraik stepped close to the cleric, saying quietly, "Father, it is urgent that I speak to you sub-rosa."

"You wish to confess?"

"I wish to inform. Where can we be closeted?"

The cleric lead the way to a small storage room off the chapel.

"Father, will you treat what I say as if it were a confession and be bound by your oath not to speak of it to any man?"

The cleric nodded. Padraik continued, "There was an attempt made on the life of the prince last night. The assassin found a dummy in the place of the prince. It was this dummy which you saw this morn, with a knife plunged into it. By great fortune I had deduced that such an attempt would be made. The prince was safe in my bed. I did not wish to alarm the child by telling him the truth. I said it was a game, a joke we played on you. Father, it was no joke. There is someone in this castle who would destroy the little prince."

The cleric looked saddened and wearied, "I had prayed that this not be true, but I had sensed a danger to the child. That is why I so readily accepted the deception as the truth. It was what I have been prepared to find."

"Father, will you help me save the boy?"

"As I serve God, yes!"

"Can you take on the responsibility of watching the boy by day for the next two days? When King Alfred arrives, the boy will have protection enough."

"I will try. Today we have the Christmas hunt. I will insist that the boy be positioned between his father and myself at all times."

"Thank you, Father John. Would you think the queen to be in danger?"

"I pray for her safety, as I do for all." If the cleric knew any threat against the queen, it was obvious that he did not intend to mention it.

The cleric returned to the chapel, followed by Padraik. Margrethe, Karyl, various courtiers and their ladies were waiting. The king and Helene entered late, their lateness delaying the beginning of the mass. Edward acquitted himself well in serving as altar boy. He had a clear voice and remembered all of the responses. Ethelred fidgeted openly, yawning and bored. He was eager to get away for breakfast and for the blood lust of the hunt.

When the company assembled to break their fast with bread and beer and sausages, Padraik managed to seat himself next to Margrethe. She asked, "What was that strange cry I heard early this morning, 'the prince is dead'?"

Padraik replied softly, "My Lady, it nearly was true. Where can we speak in private?"

"Linger for a time here at the table when the others go to prepare the hunt."

Padraik spoke loudly, asking, "What manner of hunt is this which the court goes on today?"

"All of the mounted men ride to kill game in the royal parklands. The deer or boar they kill will grace the castle table. The serfs are already out in the park, forming a huge arc of walking men, which will drive the game toward the huntsmen. They will be given any hares or other small game as their portion of the hunt."

"What plans have you for this day, my lady?"

"I would to gather mistletoe to deck the great hall for the festivities."

"Where will you go?"

"This year, I wist not. When I could see well, my ladies and an escort went with me for many leagues to find the best mistletoe." Margrethe leaned in the direction of the king, and called, "Can any tell me where the mistletoe will be found pretty and plentiful this year?"

Several suggestions were shouted back. There was noisy wrangling, then agreement that what looked to be the best supply of mistletoe could be found in the copse atop nine-stone hill.

"Nine-stone hill. My thanks," said Margrethe loudly. "Then let us plan our mistletoe hunt for nine-stone hill."

"This nine-stone hill, has it but nine stones on it?" asked Padraik.

Margrethe laughed. "No. It has its name from a circle of nine large stones in the center of the copse. These are where the druids held their festivities. Some do say that the druids also planted that copse of oak. But truly, I wist not."

Ethelred stood up and prepared to leave the table. He said, "Thomas, of the red hair, and Olfin, come, we would have speech with you in privy." Ethelred lead the way up the stairs to his chambers.

In the privy room he hoisted his robe and sat himself on the stone privy seat, grunting from the shock of the icy stone, which was chilled by the air blowing up the flue. His ermine cloak and his best wool robes hung on pegs on the opposite wall of the privy, the odors protecting them from the destruction of the moths.

"The nature of our business with you two is murder. One murder to benefit the three of us. That of Margrethe, the queen. You, Olfin, have failed us on this score once before."

"Majesty," began Olfin in self-defense, "How was I to know—"

"Enough. Be silent. The poison-dyed yarn failed. It killed, but not the right one. Time has come to be more direct. How say you, Thomas?"

"At table this morn I overheard the queen, the minnesinger, and that fool of a Karyl making plans to gather the mistletoe to deck the hall."

"Karyl is no fool, but a most valiant knight. Give him his due. What is your plan?"

"I plan that brigands shall set upon them as they are in the copse. All three shall be killed. There will be none to carry tales back."

"Then make ready as you see fit. We'll know nothing of it whilst leading the Christmas hunt. Our boy will ride with us. Keep your murderous plots away from him."

Thomas felt an inner startle of guilt. How and what could Ethelred know? "Majesty—" he began.

"Enough. We are finished," Ethelred moved from the privy seat. "Relieve yourselves to your comfort as you wish. We are going now to bestir the hunt to action." He left Olfin and Thomas in the privy.

When most of the court had left the breakfast table, Margrethe, Karyl, and Padraik sat together. Padraik whispered hurriedly, "Your son was nearly murdered last night. If I had not smelled a plot and moved him into my bed, he would now be dead."

"The king was not the viper who produced that venom," said Margrethe, "He truly loves the boy."

"Then perhaps the lad will be safe until your father comes, but you, my lady, will not."

"You think me in danger—why?"

"Think you that Alfred the king will look kindly on the way in which you are demeaned and ridiculed in this court? He will exact retribution from those who have caused hurt to you. Therefore, we are certain that your enemies mean to make way with you before your father comes."

"But what can I do? Where can I go?"

Karyl answered, "I have long considered the problem. My fief, as you know, adjoins the crown lands on the west side. A few leagues in, there is a gamekeeper's hut. I have stocked this hut to use in an emergency. It must be your refuge, if we live to get you there."

Margrethe started to speak, but Karyl silenced her. "We have no time to argue here. When you dress to gather the mistletoe, wear as many of your gowns as possible, one above the other. Small clothes the same. Wear sturdy, rough buskins and not your dainty shoes. Take two cloaks if possible. If any do question say that you feel the cold keenly these days. I go to tell the grooms to prepare our steeds."

Padraik lead Margrethe to the stairs, and went up with her to get his own cloak. It seemed to him an interminable time that he had to wait while she dressed. At last she rapped at his door.

"How do I look?"

"My lady looks to have gained a stone. Are you warm?"

"Roasting!"

They descended the stairs. "Take me to the doorway on the right," directed Margrethe. "Then through this way to the next doorway. That will be the large larder room. I must get a basket for the mistletoe."

Padraik stood in the larder room, feeling foolish, as two maids scurried around to do the queen's bidding. Between them they found a large enough slat basket to please Margrethe. Into it they placed oat cakes wrapped in a linen napkin and a small skin of wine. Padraik gladly accepted the burden of the basket. He lead Margrethe through the outer door toward the stables.

Karyl had Margrethe's fat, gentle dapple-gray palfrey standing ready to mount outside the stable door. He came through the door leading his black charger, ready to ride. Padraik went in to get Small John. He found the donkey rested and frisky, eager to get out into the clean air. Padraik saddled him quickly. They found Karyl very disgusted. "The hunters and harriers have taken all of the weapons from the armory. They left nothing except some light lances used for tilting."

"Then we must need make do with what they left," said Margrethe.

Karyl selected the best of the lances. He wore his own broadsword. Except for their bodkins, Margrethe and Padraik had no weapons. Not much to defend the trio against what was certain to be a most determined attack against them.

They set off for nine-stone hill, Karyl in the lead, followed by Margrethe balancing the basket before her saddle, with Padraik in the rear.

The sun had come out bright, if not warm, and the snowy landscape glittered and sparkled in the clear air. Padraik could not refrain from singing. He burst into a hymn of praise, then began an old ballad, in which Margrethe joined. Karyl added a deep baritone. Singing together was a joy for the moment.

The land over which they rode sloped up gently toward the central peak of nine-stone hill. They paused to look back toward the castle.

"Can you see anyone following?" asked Margrethe anxiously.

Karyl shaded his eyes against the snow glare. "I think I can just make out two men riding out the main gate now. So small they look like dark dots. We should hurry our pace a bit now, and get to the copse well before those two arrive."

There was no more singing, as they rode toward the hilltop, and the steepness increased sharply. Once they had gained the copse, Karyl urged them on into the middle of the oak grove. Here the gorse and brambles grew thick enough to make a natural barrier against horses. Karyl tethered the animals. He said, "Part of our defense must be an appearance of ignorance of any threat or danger to us. Let us go out now, and show ourselves as unsuspecting lambs awaiting the wolves."

Karyl walked slowly over the rough ground, leading Margrethe, who carried the basket. Padraik brought the lance. When they reached the outer edge of the copse the two pursuers looked much larger. Margrethe offered the wine and oat cakes to the men, but they refused. Padraik made a show of using the lance to knock a large growth of mistletoe from a tree. As he was putting it in the basket he noticed that one of the men was coming straight up their trail, and the other had started traveling around the hill to the left.

"What do you make of that, Karyl?" asked Padraik.

"I think the one coming up the frontside is meant to make us forget that the other man will be trying to surprise us from the rear. His road is longer, and he will be slower in reaching us. This way may work to our advantage. We can deal with them one at a time."

"I have an idea," said Padraik. "Can you support the weight of the lance, my lady?" Margrethe nodded. Padraik continued, "Let's set the lance with its butt against an oak. All you have to do is hold it at this angle. If Karyl and I stand out in front of it, thusly, it will mask the danger of the lance from that horseman. When he is almost upon us, Karyl and I will jump aside. With luck the horse will impale itself on the lance. As it hits the lance, my lady, the lance will likely be pulled from your hands by the force. When this happens, you get back behind the tree."

"Good strategy," said Karyl. "You should have been a commander of armies, not a minnesinger. Are you ready, now, my queen? Here comes his charge."

Margrethe heard the rush of hooves as the horseman dashed straight at Karyl and Padraik. Padraik shouted, "Now!" and he jumped left as Karyl went to the right. The horseman was unable to turn his horse before it ran into the lance point, which entered its breast. Hard hurt, the horse began to scream. Margrethe covered her ears to shut out the sound. The rider had been unseated by the shock, and Karyl slashed off his head without compunction.

Now there was only the enemy approaching from the rear. As Karyl entered the copse the enemy came at him on the run. Due to his knightly training, Karyl automatically flung up his shield arm to deflect the blow, forgetting that he had no shield. The sword of his assailant slashed Karl's left upper arm to the bone. With a cry of hurt and anger, Karyl slashed straight into the belly of the assailant. Padraik ran up behind the enemy and stabbed him in the heart. The man dropped dead without further struggle. Karyl collapsed against the trunk of an oak tree from relief and weariness. Blood was pouring freely from his wounded arm.

"Quickly, my lady, give me your wimple," called Karyl.

"Here is the napkin from the oatcakes," offered Margrethe.

"No! Your wimple. Hurry. I bleed too well."

Margrethe pulled off her head cloth and Karyl pressed it firmly against his wound. The bleeding continued, but at a slower rate as he kept the pressure steady.

"I could use some of that wine now," Karyl said.

Padraik brought him the wineskin and steadied it against his lips.

"My thanks. Help me to sit."

Padraik helped Karyl lower himself to the ground. Karyl leaned his head back against the tree, his face very white, his eyes closed. Padraik left him to rest and went to dispatch the wounded horse, which was still groaning and whickering in agony. He used Karyl's broadsword to slash the animal's throat. The resulting quiet came pleasantly to the ears.

Karyl had his eyes open when Padraik walked back to him. "Better refresh yourself, too," said Karyl, "Our battle is but half done."

Padraik and Margrethe drank of the wine and ate an oat cake each. Karyl refused to eat, but asked for more wine. After Padraik had assisted him again to drink, Karyl said, "Now we must rid ourselves of these bodies and get the queen to sanctuary. Then you and I must return to the castle to report that we have been attacked, and the queen abducted. Have you seen anything of the mount belonging to the fellow who wounded me?"

Padraik went in search of the animal and found it standing near Karyl's charger. It had recognized its stablemate. Padraik spoke soothingly to the horse as he picked up its bridle rein and lead it to Karyl. Karyl moved stiffly to his feet. "Now may I have that napkin, my lady?" Margrethe moved near enough that she could see his wounded arm. She took the bloodied wimple from the cut, and bound the linen napkin into place, tying it firmly.

"What can I do now?" asked Padraik.

"Collect the remains of that first dastard, Olfin. Find some way to keep his head with his body, and tie them onto the horse. This other fellow was Tom, brother to Helene. The same one, in certainty, that instigated the attack on our little prince."

Margrethe gave a gasp of amazed disbelief.

Padraik took the saddlecloth from the horse to use to wrap the body and head together. He tied the bundle to the horse, who skittered and shied, not liking the smell of blood.

"Now add the other body across the back of the horse. Use his belt to attach his hands and feet together under the horses belly. That's good enough. We must travel a full two leagues to the sea cliff."

"My lady," Karyl called. Margrethe leaned near him. He put up his good hand and caught her treasured Tuscan beads. With a firm jerk he broke the string, scattering globes of bright blue glass over the snow.

Margrethe cried, "No!"

"Yes, my lady," said Karyl. "It must look as if we were attacked and put up a strong resistance before you were abducted. Now drop that bloody wimple on the clan snow on the other side of this tree."

Margrethe did so.

"Time has come for us to go. Give me more of the wine." Karyl drained all of the wine. Padraik assisted Margrethe to mount, which was not difficult. He held the black charger so that Karyl could mount. Then he got patient Small John. Leading the horse with the two bodies, Padraik mounted on Small John followed Karyl who guided them to the sea cliff. No person noticed them as they rode. Once they had arrived at the cliff, Padraik went cautiously to the verge to look down. The tide was in, with waves leaping halfway up the sheer rock face. Nothing to stop the bodies from going straight down into the water.

Padraik rode back to report this to Karyl, who said, "Good. There should be nothing to stop a live horse either, should there?"

They rode nearer to the cliff edge . Suddenly Karyl gave a series of loud yells, and poked the body-carrying horse in the rump with his broadsword. The animal panicked into a gallop and was off the edge before it knew what was happening. The cold waves closed over its head, leaving no trace.

"So much for the expendable trash. Now to get the queen to the gamekeeper's hut on my land. We have a ride of about four leagues to get there." Karyl led the way at a fair pace, although he seemed a bit unsteady from time to time. At a boundary marker Karyl said, "This is where my fief begins and the Crown land ends. Only another league and we'll be at the hut."

The sky had clouded over, and a murky half-light filtered through the great trees as they entered the forest. The stone hut was isolated, with no other habitations for a great distance in any direction. Karyl dismounted and opened the heavy door. "Welcome to your new palace, my lady."

It seemed colder inside the hut than outside. The oaken pail of water on a shelf had frozen solid. Wood cut ready to burn was stacked neatly along one entire wall. The fireplace filled the back end of the room. On the hearthstone stood a large three-legged pot. A small kettle hung by its chains from the fireplace crane.

A fire had been laid, ready to kindle. Karyl drew an oilskin-wrapped bundle from his pouch. "Can you use the flint and steel to light the tinder?" he asked Padraik.

Padraik set to work with a practiced hand and soon had sparks glowing. Transferring them to the fireplace took much patience. The draft down the chimney would extinguish the sparks before the kindling material could catch. At last a tiny blaze was glowing in the straw and twigs. It grew, consuming the small twigs greedily and reaching up for larger food. The cheerful crackle of the fire warmed them as much by its promise as by its growing heat.

"Help me with this, Padraik," Karyl lead him to a cask on the other side of the room. "This is ale, but it hasn't been started yet. Can you knock in the bung hole? Here is the stopper."

"What do we draw the ale into?"

"Look on the shelf near the water pail."

Padraik searched, and found an earthenware beaker, a large wooden basin, a small wooden bowl, a trencher, and two wooden spoons. Selecting the beaker and the large basin Padraik took them to the ale cask. He used a billet of wood as the driving force needed to hammer out the bung hole.

The ale foamed out onto the floor before he had the basin in place. He filled the basin, and the beaker, and carried the ale to the hearth.

Margrethe was sitting on the hearthstone, toasting her back while her breath steamed on the still-frosty air of the room. She gratefully accepted the beaker of ale. Padraik and Karyl shared the basin, each drinking in turn. When they had emptied the basin Karyl said, "My lady, we must leave you now. There are foodstuffs in the row of crocks near the bedbench. Whatever you do, don't let your fire die out, or you will freeze. There are two heavy bars of wood beside the door. As soon as we have gone outside, set both of the bars into place, and do not open the door for anyone."

"There are no thanks I can give for the favor of my life. I am forever in your debt. What will you do with my palfrey?"

"She will be in the rude stable behind this hut. There is old hay, and a trough of snow-water. She will manage for a few days without care. I'll return when I can. Come, Padraik."

Padraik dropped to one knee and raised Margrethe's hand, so soft and white, to his lips. "Let God stay with you, lady," he whispered, too moved by her poignant air of helplessness to speak aloud.

Margrethe could be heard barring the door after they had closed it behind them. The men lead the palfrey to the rough stable. With saddle, bridle and trappings removed she was but an ordinary fat gray mare. She whinnied softly as they turned to leave, asking not to be left alone, but the men went anyway. They fastened securely the gate to the log fenced stableyard.

Padraik and Karyl made as much speed on their return journey as Small John could make. Even so, darkness found them still within the forest. Karyl knew the way and was well in the lead when suddenly Padraik was struck a fearsome blow on the forehead. He had ridden full-tilt into a tree limb, which laid him unconscious on the ground. Karyl had continued for almost half a league before he missed Padraik. He retraced his route and found Small John standing patiently beside the body of his owner.

"By the body of our sweet Lord, what next?" asked Karyl. He dismounted. Padraik showed no signs of life as Karyl with much pain and difficulty caused by his wound lifted him up and draped him across the back of Small John. Karyl lead the donkey, and kept his own horse to a more gentle pace as they completed their journey.

The castle was in an uproar over the missing queen. The cleric looked at Padraik, and pronounced him to be stunned, not dead. He was a better physic than he was a cleric and was happy to have a patient who could not protest his treatment.

Karyl made his report to the king, who questioned him closely.

"Did you recognize those men who set upon you?"

"No, majesty," lied Karyl. "They wore black hoods, as do executioners."

"You do not think them common brigands?"

"No, majesty. They came at us with plot and purpose. To kill ourselves and our queen. Only those who were at table with us this morning could have known where we would be found. This had to be a castle plot."

"Do you suspect anyone?"

"No one, your majesty," replied Karyl before he collapsed in a faint. The strain of his wound and the hard day were too much to bear. Karyl was carried to the infirmary and bedded beside Padraik.

Ethelred sat and pulled at his lower lip, which he did only when puzzled. There was something here which did not smell just right. Something—but what he could not tell. Time would sort it all out.

The odor of roast boar filled the great hall as four serving men came in carrying the giant trencher. Huge chunks of meat were hacked from the carcass and placed on smaller trenchers, which were set within reach of the diners. These were slid up and down the table as the hungry hunters and their ladies desired to cut a portion to eat on their bread.

A missing queen was just a missing queen. But a hungry belly demanded satisfaction.

CHAPTER 3

When Margrethe had barred the door behind Karyl and Padraik, she was suddenly aware of how tired she was. The fire was warming the room, so she dispensed with her two cloaks and removed the uppermost two gowns that she was wearing. She wondered how much wood to give the fire to keep it burning through the night. Not knowing, Margrethe piled several logs on the blaze, which was promptly reduced to smoldering. Perhaps it would go out, but she was too exhausted to cope with that problem. She stretched out on the bedbench, covered herself with the two cloaks, and was instantly asleep.

The terrors of the day invaded her dreaming. She heard again the pounding of the horses' hooves and the cries of the battle, and awakened to find the room stifling hot. All of the wood she had placed on the fire was burning at once. She watched it until the fire had diminished somewhat, then added one more log and went back to sleep.

The room had cooled, and morning was well advanced when next she awoke. Margrethe was aware of how sore and stiff her muscles were as she arose to give the fire another feeding. She was hungry. Karyl had said that there was food in the crocks near the bedbench. She felt her way gingerly to them, then knelt down so that the contents of the crocks would be within her range of vision. She found that one crock held dried peas, one had lentils, one was full of wheat corns, and the last held dried apple slices. She nibbled one of the apple slices while she pondered the problem of how to cook her food. She could not help laughing at her own predicament.

"Poor helpless wight," she said aloud. "You have wit enough to know that you are hungry, but not wit enough to know how to cook, even with plenty of foodstuffs at hand."

Margrethe had never even watched the food preparations in the castle kitchens. Determined not to be defeated by her ignorance, she half-filled the small kettle with water and hung it on the crane over the fire. To this she added a bowlful of dried peas. Trusting that those would soon be done, she felt her way to the ale cask. The stopper bung was almost beyond her strength to remove, but she managed to draw herself a beaker of ale without spilling an undue amount. She got a handful of the dried apple slices and sat down to await the cooking of the peas. It was plain, thought Margrethe, that until she gained some skill in cookery her meals would be eaten whenever the food got done.

Padraik opened his eyes to find Edward looking at him. The child looked troubled. "Can you hear me, Padraik?" he asked.

Padraik started to nod, which made his head ache most fiercely.

"Padraik, you didn't wake up all yesterday. My grandfather has already come. He came in and looked at you, but you just slept." The child giggled, "You do look so funny with that big lump on your forehead, and such black circles around your eyes."

"Don't feel funny, feel terrible," muttered Padraik.

"Grandfather and some of his knights and my father have all gone out to nine-stone hill to see if they can trace where the brigands took Mother."

"Didn't Karyl tell what happened?" asked Padraik.

"He said some. Then he fainted away like one of the court ladies at a tourney. Had to be carried in here. If you turn your head this way you can see him."

Although the movement made him groan with pain, Padraik turned his head enough to see Karyl. He lay red of face and muttering on the next cot. His injured arm was covered by a dirty bandage, through which pus was seeping.

"Grandfather says when he returns he will have Karyl properly attended."

Padraik's eye movements seemed to increase the intensity of his headache. "Is Father John here?" he asked.

"He will be back quickly. He gave me the task of watching over you until he could return."

Padraik closed his eyes. The pain put him out of touch with reality. He was jolted back into sudden awareness when a voice said, "Here I am, my son."

"Please, Father, too much pain! Is there any poppy juice?"

"In this cup of wine. Drink it down. For heads hurt like yours, sleep is good."

Padraik eagerly drained the opium-laced wine. Almost immediately he began to drift in and out of consciousness. When King Alfred returned he found Padraik deep in drugged sleep.

The returning King Alfred was greeted gleefully by his grandson. The boy ran and grabbed him by the hand saying, "Grandsire, did you find any trace of Old Red-Eyes?"

"Whom do you mean, lad?" asked Alfred.

"Old red-eyed Margrethe," said Edward.

Alfred cuffed the boy sharply, "That's no way to refer to your royal mother."

Edward's eyes filled with tears as he said, "But that's what he calls her," pointing at his father.

Ethelred quickly responded, "Only in jest, sire, only in jest."

Alfred regarded his son-in-law with suspicion. His suspicions deepened when the trestle table was set up for supper. The high chair beside Ethelred was empty. Edward glanced around the room and asked, "Why isn't Helene eating beside you, as she always does, Father?"

"That seat by right belongs to your mother," said Alfred.

"But Old Red—uh, my mother, always sits down at the far end of the table. Ever since she got the poison in her eyes and can't see very good."

"What is this about our daughter's eyes?" asked Alfred.

"She used some yarn which had been dyed with a poisonous dye to complete that great tapestry there. She rubbed the poison into her eyes, and it destroyed most of her sight. She was also ill afterward, and was more comfortable with a seat nearer to the fire," explained Ethelred, glaring at his son, who looked away innocently.

"Why was I not informed?" demanded Alfred.

"The cleric wrote at her behest. Did you not receive the messages?"

"No messages came. Conditions on the high roads are not always to the benefit of the traveler, but few would dare to interfere with a royal messenger. Who is your messenger?"

"Olfin. He is away on business for us now."

"Will this Olfin be returning soon?"

"That we cannot say. He had orders to see that some uncompleted work was finished before he returned." Ethelred was uncomfortable thinking about what could have transpired with Olfin, Thomas, and the queen. There was not much evidence at the site of the ambush, save for Olfin's dead horse, Margrethe's bloody wimple, and broken blue beads. With luck, Margrethe had been disposed of forever. Ethelred most earnestly hoped so. He desired to get on with marrying Helene, so that his new son would not be born a bastard.

By the fourth day of living in the gamekeeper's hut, Margrethe had memorized the positions of the simple furnishings of the hut. This made moving about much less complicated. She had also learned how much and how often to feed the fire. Cooking was still a matter of trial and error. She could not find salt to season what she cooked.

Margrethe had really expected that Karyl would return by the fourth day. She unbarred the door and went carefully, feeling along the wall for support, to the stableyard. Her palfrey heard her coming, and set up a delighted nickering. Margrethe petted and stroked the mare, very glad herself to have another creature to talk to. The mare seemed to be in good condition.

Margrethe turned to leave and stumbled over a soft, feathery ball. She knelt down to see what she had stumbled over, and found a young owl with a broken wing. It fluttered and struggled as she picked it up, crooning, "There, there, my sweeting. Margrethe will care for you." She cuddled the owl to her breast as she made her way back to the warm haven of the hut. Margrethe cut a thick sliver of wood from a batten and tore a strip of cloth from a kerchief. Holding the resistant owl between her knees, she splinted the wing neatly. When she had finished, the owl stopped struggling and regarded her solemnly with his round eyes. "I'm going to call you William," Margrethe said. "Because when my brother William was a baby he used to stare at me with just such big round eyes." She set the newly christened William on the floor near the ale keg. William pulled his head down, ruffled up his feathers, closed his eyes, and was soon asleep.

Margrethe puzzled about what to feed an owl. Water all creatures must have. She used the shallow trencher to hold the water. If William should refuse the wheat, lentils, and peas there would be no food for him. She placed a small amount of each on the floor near him, to see which he would prefer.

After his nap, William showed his scorn for the food. He flicked it around his area with beak and feet, and set up an angry chuttering when Margrethe came and knelt to see what he was doing. William nipped at her fingers.

"Poor creature!" said Margrethe. "Poor creature. I would give you flesh to eat, had I aught. Poor hungry William. I'm hungry, too, but I eat what I have. I do crave meat in a most fervent way. But there is no meat for either of us." She laughed ruefully, "William, so unfitted for living here am I that even if a fat healthy young, hare should come and obligingly die upon the doorstep, we would still not have meat. I have no knowledge of how to remove the skin and entrails of a hare. Nor of how to cook it if it came ready skinned and gutted. Nothing I have ever learned in my life has a use here. I was taught to be skillful with a needle, to embroider, to weave, to spin, to design a tapestry. I can play a lute and sing sweetly. I can make polite converse with royalty, make gay badinage to lighten the mood of company. The skills of which I am now in need, I have not. Lord Jesu have mercy!"

Much disgruntled, William settled to sleep again.

During, the night a mouse came down from the thatch of the roof to collect some of the food William had scorned. William's sharp ears had detected the approach of the mouse, who was unaware of the owl until it was seized. There was one shrill squeal from the mouse, then only the crunch and gulp of William's dining. He gave a satisfied chortle.

Margrethe, awake on the bedbench, could tell by the sounds what had occurred. "Thanks be to thee, Lord, for providing for the bird. Please thou to have mercy on me," she prayed.

One of King Alfred's knights had much skill in treating battle wounds. He was glad to tend Karyl's injury. He threw away the soiled bandage the cleric had used, cleansed the wound well with a saline solution, and applied an ointment of his own secret manufacture. Then he bound up the arm lightly with clean cloths. Karyl's fever began to retreat swiftly. He was able to sit up in bed and speak lucidly with King Alfred on the following morrow.

What Karyl had to tell about the attack was very little. It was obvious that both Karyl and Padraik had been wounded, and the queen and the two assailants had just disappeared. King Alfred was not satisfied.

Padraik was having less pain each day and spending more time awake. As soon as Padraik was steady enough on his legs to walk unaided, King Alfred requested a private conversation. They found a secluded corner in the castle.

"Now tell us truly, as you are pledged to our service, what is this tangle of lies which hides the truth about our daughter?" asked the king.

"You think we lie to you, your majesty?"

"Certes! And not too well. If Queen Margrethe were dead, you would be filled with grief. If she had been truly taken by brigands, you would not be content until the dastards had been discovered and slain."

"Your majesty is shrewd. Does King Ethelred suspect?"

"No. That one is too full of himself and his own desires."

"Your Majesty, I place the life of the good knight Karyl in jeopardy when I tell you this. Your royal daughter was much dishonored in this court. Her life, and the life of her son, have both been endangered by the ambitions of the harlot. Karyl's wife was gentlewoman to the queen until she had an accident and fell to her death. Karyl has ever been faithful to Margrethe, her true knight, ever gentle and courteous during her times of trouble. He was much concerned for her safekeeping. Karyl could see, as could I, that this visit from you would draw the brewing troubles to a head. He had prepared a place of refuge. After we were set upon by the two murderers we got her safely there."

"And the murderers?"

"Both dead and in the ocean."

"Brigands, do you think?"

"Nay, Majesty, they were of this court. Olfin, sometime messenger for the king, and Thomas, brother to Helene the harlot. They must have been doing the bidding of the king.

As you would value the life of your daughter, pretend to accept her death as fact. Otherwise, King Ethelred has many unscrupulous men in his pay who would be happy to search out her hiding place and kill her for a very small sum of money."

"To save her alive, then, we must declare our daughter dead. And the boy, he is in danger, also?"

"Your majesty, I was able to foil one attempt on his life. He will never be safe here, because he is the true heir to the throne."

King Alfred began to pace up and down restlessly. "How could we have been so deceived when choosing a husband for our daughter? Ethelred made such a good show as a suitor, and it seemed wise to ally our two kingdoms by marriage. And now our daughter is as lost to us as if she were truly dead. In such a situation what can we do?"

"Mourn her as dead, and let her have a chance to live. Karyl will protect her as far as a mortal can. The fact that you are taking Prince Edward away for his fosterage will save him."

✠ ✠ ✠

When the next day dawned King Alfred called up his knights. "Today we travel. The weather has held too fair to trust. We must go this day or risk being stormbound." The knights gave the word to their attendants, and the occupants of the castle stirred into a bustle of activity while Alfred went to speak with Ethelred.

"We will take your son for his fosterage, as we agreed to do at his birth. It is well that this comes at the time when he has just lost his mother. It is always difficult for a lad to adjust to his foster home. Now Edward can get over the loss of his mother and his infant home at the same time."

"We will miss our son," said Ethelred, "but it is time he learned to be a man. He has been overlong among the court ladies, and is soft as a girl. Has no stomach for wine at all."

"Of course, now that the queen, our daughter, is dead, we will require her jewel casket from you."

"Her jewel casket?" asked King Ethelred.

"Yes. With all of the jewels. They compose an entailed inheritance, to go to the heirs of her body. They came to our daughter through her mother and grandmother. Now they must go to Edward."

"Oh. We see. We have no idea where those jewels might be."

"It would be well if they were found, and quickly. If it would aid you, my men can assist in searching the castle for the jewels," said Alfred.

"No need, no need. Perhaps we can recall where Margrethe kept the jewel casket."

"Had she no attendants? She brought two ladies with her, and added two more here."

"Alas, three have died. Only the fourth, Helene, is still here."

"Then we would think it well to have Helene find the jewels."

King Alfred walked away, leaving a confounded Ethelred to pull at his lower lip and wonder how to cope with Helene.

A furious Helene finally gave up the jewels to Ethelred. "You promised those gems to me!" she protested.

"Nay. We promised to wed you. We will. There were no jewels mentioned." He checked the contents of the jewel casket. "Where are the rubies?"

"Are they not there, my lord?"

"Well you know that they are not. Where are they?" Ethelred grabbed Helene's shoulder roughly, pulling the neck of her gown away. This revealed the golden chain of the ruby necklace. She wept as he took the jewels from her, but to no avail.

"These are our son's heritage from his mother. It is right that he have them."

Ethelred was glad to be rid of the casket when he placed it in Alfred's hands. Alfred thanked him after a cursory glance at the contents.

Edward's meager belongings were gathered together, and the cavalcade of travelers was ready to set off. One king on his huge gray destrier, one prince on a pony, one minnesinger on a donkey led the procession of forty knights at arms, twenty bowmen, equerries, and grooms all mounted on sleek horses made a brave show on the cold first day of January as they exited through the main castle gate. Once through the castle village they turned north, on the road to Dorchester, where they would spend the night.

CHAPTER 4

The severe winter storm that hit the kingdom of Wessex on the second day of January made captives of both men and beasts. The blizzard raged for three days—the worst storm in living memory. Wind-driven snow piled high in lane and field, smoothing out the sharp contours of the land.

Inside the gamekeeper's hut Margrethe and William felt the increasing chill of the outside air, even though the fire still blazed merrily on the hearth. Margrethe pushed her benchbed nearer to the fire. William, who did not like being near the fireplace at first, came nearer as frost began to form in the corners of the room farthest from the heat. The water in the oaken bucket was almost gone. What little was left froze solid. Margrethe had to set the pail on the hearth to melt enough water for her simple cooking. What would she do when the water was gone? Surely, Karyl would arrive at any time. This thought carried her through this period of trial.

On the morning of the fourth day, the wind no longer screamed around the hut. Margrethe unbarred the door and pulled it open to see snow drifted as high as her shoulders against the hut. She filled the water pail with snow, saying a quick *Deo gratias*. Had she realized how much snow was needed to make enough water to fill the small kettle, she might not have been quite so grateful.

William began to be very restless after the end of the storm. He was trying to stretch and flap his injured wing. It evidently no longer gave him any pain. He chittered and fussed for so long before the door late one afternoon that Margrethe opened the door to show him the drifted snow. William still wanted out. Against her better judgment, she unbound his splinted wing and lifted him up above the level of the snowbank. William gave a powerful leap and soared up away from her protective hands.

Margrethe closed the door, sat down, and was overcome by a sense of loss. Releasing William back into his wild world seemed to release all of the dammed-up tears in Margrethe. She wept for her son, now gone to his foster home; for her husband, whose heart had turned against her; for her father, whom she longed to see; and for herself, half-blind and stumbling along from day to day as best she could, hoping always for the arrival of Karyl. When finally she had no more tears to shed, she mopped her face and blew her red nose. She chided herself, *Margrethe, Margrethe, you never learned to weep like a queen, or even like a lady. A noble woman sheds genteel tears, and looks sweetly pathetic, while you always sob like an injured child, and your nose gets all red and swollen.* She was glad to have had no witness to her grief and set her supper kettle on to cook.

That night Margrethe missed William. The young owl had been company for her. Margrethe had scarcely risen the next morning when a thump sounded on the door. Hopeful that it might be Karyl, she hastened to unbar the door. Before she had the bars off there came another thump. She opened the door to find not Karyl but William pounding at the door with his beak. William gave one shuddering call, "Who-hu-hu-hu-huff," and flapped up onto the shelf that held Margrethe's tableware. He looked well, and his soft abdomen was distended. Obviously he had found good hunting. Margrethe touched his head gently, and William closed his eyes to sleep in his haven of safety.

Much cheered by William's return, Margrethe took thought for her palfrey. Had the mare survived the blizzard? She thought that she could hear the mare in her stableyard, now that the wind had quieted. She wished for a stave, or even just a long tree branch that she could use for testing the snow. Without such an aid, she dared not attempt to go back to the stable. She also wished for some wooden pattens to keep her shoes from being soaked by the snow.

✞   ✞   ✞

Karyl was still at Torr Castle. The blizzard had delayed his return to Margrethe. During the days when all of the world had been snowbound, Karyl had approached Ethelred.

"Your majesty, I request permission to leave the court for a time, and return to my own fief."

"You are not happy with us?" asked Ethelred.

"I feel too deeply shamed by my failure to protect your royal dame. Now she is gone forever, and that is a daily reminder of my defeat by those evil men who took her."

"You did your best. You did not fail our command. When do you desire to go?"

"As soon as the roads permit travel. My wound is healing, and my strength is well returned."

"Our royal decision is this. Wait until we are married to Helene. We wish all of our nobles to witness this event. Then you are free to leave us for a time. We have spoken." Ethelred walked away, leaving Karyl to plan his journey.

Father John had made mild protest over the impending wedding of Ethelred and Helene. Ethelred was rudely short with Father John, who said no more. Instead, Father John spent long hours praying in the icy chapel. At last he thought he heard an answer from God. A tiny voice inside his own mind said, *Little man, save yourself by doing the king's bidding. For if you are no longer there, who would serve Me in the castle?*

Father John prepared for the nuptial mass. He missed young Edward. The lad had made a good altar boy, even with all his mischievous tricks. Edward had been a ray of sunshine in the gloomy castle.

Helene had ordered that a huge feast be prepared for the wedding breakfast. The castle kitchens were in an uproar, crowded with helpers brought in from the castle village. For her wedding gown Helene wore red, the color of joy. Ethelred was roughly protective of her. If any of the nobles thought that this wedding was less than proper, they were wise enough not to speak.

The company attended the mass. Ceremony out of the way, they attacked the feast. They ate and drank themselves into insensibility. Slept a bit, sobered some, and returned to the table to eat and drink again. They sang all the bawdy songs loved by the king, made broad jokes, mixed up their bedmates, and enjoyed the license given by the occasion. Karyl remained as aloof as possible, pleading a weakness from his recent wound.

Helene drank heartily, but ate little. The child was so active inside her, kicking and bumping lustily, that she found it difficult to eat. She had one pleasing thought: *Queen at last! Now I shall have fine furs, and jewels. I am Queen Helene.* She nuzzled the king, who responded with delighted ardor. And drank. And drank.

The third day after the ending of the storm Karyl left the confines of the castle. His charger was fresh and well rested. The cold air caused it to frisk like a colt. Karyl turned west, and was soon on the road to his own fief.

On that morning Margrethe was awakened by definite sounds from the stable. Her palfrey set up a protesting neighing, and a man was shouting loudly. Startled, she slipped into her two cloaks and opened the door of the hut. She had reached the corner of the hut when an outlaw came from the stableyard, leading her mare. The outlaw was dressed in multiple layers of ragged garments, his feet bound in strips of hide. When he saw Margrethe, his face brightened with delight. His mouth revealed stumps of rotting teeth as he said, "Luk, naow at the wrench. Alone here, be ye? Whar be tha man?"

Margrethe could scarcely make sense of his words in her terror. She turned to run, but in two steps the outlaw had seized her arm. He dragged her toward the open door of the hut. After glancing around suspiciously inside, he pulled Margrethe in the door. She struggled to free herself, which angered him. He struck her in the face, and she gave a frightened shriek.

Just then William returned from his night of hunting. Seeing the door was open, he flew straight in, one wingtip brushing the face of the surprised man. Then he gave his usual "Who-hu-hu-hu-huff," as he settled on the shelf.

"Witch!" spat the outlaw. "Witch, and ye called tha familiar. Ah'll have naught o'ye." He ran from the hut, mounted the palfrey, and bolted down the road toward the highway.

Margrethe was trembling so hard from terror that she found closing and barring the door difficult. Fortunately the fire needed tending, and she calmed a bit while working with it. She hung her small kettle of water and wheat on the crane to cook over the fire and sat down. The horror of the incident swept back over her. She felt soiled just from his touch, and when she realized what he probably wanted with her she became nauseated. To think that her gentle palfrey was in the hands of such a creature! She drew herself some ale, and was sipping it when there came a pounding on the door.

Margrethe was too terrified to open it. The pounding was repeated. Then a voice calling, "My lady, are you in there? Open up, it's Karyl."

Margrethe fumbled with the bars of the door. Karyl, Karyl back at last! Finally the door opened. He stepped inside. "Are you well, my lady?" Margrethe could only lean against his chest and nod in reply. All would be well, now that Karyl had returned. But he was so thin! The fire of the fever had burned away all of the fat from his tissues. He looked anxious, and his sword hand was covered with blood. Margrethe examined his hand with some concern.

Karyl laughed shortly. "That gore isn't mine. It is from an outlaw. I saw him tearing down the road toward me, riding your palfrey. I called to him to halt, and he paid no heed. So I blocked his way, determined that he really was an outlaw and not some hapless villein, and killed him."

"Oh, I am glad," whispered Margrethe, "I am glad! He came in here to dishonor me, but William saved me."

"William?" asked Karyl, looking blank.

Margrethe laughed, "Yes, William. Here he is." She went to the shelf and stroked the owl softly. He blinked his eyes once, and returned to sleep. "Because of William flying in at the door, the outlaw thought me a witch. He was frightened, calling William my familiar, and he rode away on my palfrey as fast as she would go. How is she?"

"She? Oh, your mare. Good. I put her in the stableyard with my charger." He sniffed the air, "What are you burning?"

"Wood, of course!"

"No, in the kettle."

"Oh, my wheat!" Margrethe hastily swung the crane away from the fire. She added a little more water to the kettle. "Will you share my breakfast? I think the wheat to be but slightly scorched."

Karyl had broken his fast at the castle, but he accepted a small portion of the boiled wheat.

"Where did you leave the salt?" asked Margrethe.

"Salt? Oh, I forgot to provide salt. Sorry. I had never thought to leave you here alone for so long, and with such meager fare. However, I was most dreadfully ill with poisoning of my wound. Had it not been for the skill of one of your father's knights I would not be above ground now. The illness, the storm, and your husband's marriage all delayed my return."

"Marriage? Oh, of course, Helene and her bastard. I wonder how Ethelred would think the child his when it could belong to any of a dozen?" Margrethe sat in silent thought. "Karyl, do you think me guilty of sin?" she asked.

"You? My lady, you have been much sinned against!"

"But I am guilty. Because I have run and hid myself, my husband has made a bigamous marriage. I think it sure that God will lay his sin to my charge. Had I but accepted my fate gracefully my husband would not now be living in sin."

"Fair Margrethe, killing you would have been far worse sin."

"Mayhap. At any rate, 'tis done. I have thought much about it while here alone."

"You've been too much alone. You need a sturdy companion, one with strong limbs and young eyes. Would you object to a maid whose face is disfigured? There is such a one working in the kitchen of my manor house. She was born with the mark of the burning brand on one side of her face. The other side is fair enough. This girl, who is called Rose, was cast out by her family because of the birthmark. I took her into my service as a tiny child to save her life. The village children taunt and torment her, but for all that, she is a sweet enough person."

"Where will she sleep? I have but one bed."

"A blanket near the fire will be comfort for her."

"There is no blanket."

"Indeed there are blankets."

"Where? I found none."

"In the kist of your benchbed." Karyl removed the thin mattress and raised a lid. "See? four warm blankets. How have you kept warm at night?"

"By covering with both my cloaks. It will be good to use these blankets." Margrethe removed them from the kist.

"I did not know of the kist. I did not know many things. Where do I get water?"

"That will be a task for Rose. The stream is at least a furlong away through the woods. The stream is swift and normally does not freeze in winter." Karyl walked around inside the hut, making an inventory of what would be needed. He would bring some dried smoked fish when he returned with Rose, as well as salt and other supplies.

Margrethe suddenly thought to ask about Padraik. She was much dismayed to learn of his accident. Karyl reassured her that Padraik was quite recovered in time to depart from the castle with King Alfred, Prince Edward, and the court from Sussex.

"That is well," Margrethe smiled. "Padraik was ever a source of joy to me as a child. Glad I am that my own son has now the pleasure of growing up in his company. Do you think that one day Padraik may come to visit me here?"

"I think it likely, my lady, that he should want to do so. It may well be that he would not know how to find the way alone. I will find a way to communicate with him. Now I must go, if I am to return before nightfall with Rose."

Karyl rode away, leaving a much contented Margrethe. It looked as if the worst of her problems had ended.

CHAPTER 5

King Alfred and his retinue had reached the town of Dorchester before the great blizzard. A fast courier had been sent on ahead so that the ruler of the castle could prepare for the impending visit. This ruler, Earl Axel, was first cousin to Ethelred. Edward had often heard of his castle in Dorchester. He was surprised to find that it was not as large as his own home. It was square and sturdy, with a rounded tower at each corner. The castle yard was too small to be a real tournament yard.

Earl Axel and his consort, Gwynna, kept a happy, sociable court. Their two sons, Paul and Arthur, were respectively two and three years older than Edward. Though they were his first cousins, once removed, Edward had never met the boys before. Axel and Gwynna had always left their sons at home when they had visited.

Edward wanted to approach his cousins in a friendly manner, but was uncertain as to how to behave. He had never had playmates near his own age. He clung closely to the side of King Alfred.

"Run along now, and play with your cousins," ordered Alfred, giving the child a little shove.

The three boys stood and looked at each other like strange puppies, undecided on whether to romp or to fight.

"Want to play ball?" asked Paul. Edward nodded, and the boys went into a hallway where they had placed markings along the walls for their games. Paul and Arthur ran and threw the ball with abandon, according to rules that were totally incomprehensible to Edward. He ran at the wrong time, threw the ball in the wrong manner, and finally gave up in total disgust.

Edward felt disgruntled as he went to find his grandfather. Hearing the other boys laughing and playing heartily without him only added to his unhappiness.

"Grandsire, I can't play their game," he said to Alfred.

"Then you must learn. That is a part of growing up into your manhood. Every game has rules that the players must learn. Every player must abide by the rules, or be a knave. That is life, Edward."

"Why must life be so hard, grandsire?"

"If we knew the reason for that we would be as wise as God." Alfred smiled at the overly serious child. "Find Padraik. Ask him to teach you the riddle song about the catkins."

Padraik kept the boy distracted for the remainder of the day. Edward loved the riddle songs, and was delighted to learn a new one. He went back to find his cousins, singing the new song as he went.

> *Riddle me ree, riddle me rye,*
> *A riddle, a riddle, a riddle have I,*
> *Of ten catkins hanging so high.*
> *Can you, or you, or you tell why?*

The riddle song gave Edward instant popularity with the other boys. They gave him no peace of mind until he agreed to teach them this new song also.

The big storm kept everyone indoors with its fury. During this time, Edward had his first chance to observe genteel behavior by a whole court. The court ladies amused themselves with fine stitchery while playing word games, which included some very intricate word puzzles. The men gamed with dice, and bet on Jack's Alive, while sharpening their weapons and talking. In the evening Padraik was called on to tell stories to the company, and he gave them strange tales from many lands. Dorchester Castle kept a trio of court musicians, who furnished music for dancing. The dancing was primarily contra dance, with the women in one row facing the men in another row. Edward was entranced. His small feet beat time to the music. He could see that here, too, were rules to be learned. Each dancer moved according to a set pattern. It made for order and beauty in the dancing. Edward watched until he fell asleep.

At Dorchester Edward shared a room with Padraik. The boy was ever full of questions at bedtime.

"Why is your donkey called Small John?" he asked.

"Because your grandfather's destrier is named Great John," replied Padraik with a twinkle. "Had I but called the donkey John people might have confused the two animals."

"Why must there be fosterage for boys like me?"

"Because one day you will be king. It is necessary that you live away from home and learn the ways of various peoples."

"Why don't Paul and Arthur go away from their home?"

"They will soon. It was not needful that they begin their training as early as you. They will be but cousins to the king."

"Oh Padraik," yawned the child, "I didn't know there was so much to learn, nor so many new things in all this world." His head nodded. He did not protest as Padraik guided him in getting himself ready for bed. Padraik thought Edward to be asleep until a drowsy voice said, "Padraik, haven't I learned much already?"

Karyl returned to Margrethe as he had promised, with Rose riding pillion behind him, clinging to his waist. Karyl was loading a heavily laden pack horse. Among the items on the pack horse was the salt Margrethe needed. He had brought some smoked fish as well. He brought additional utensils, including a quern. There was also a bag of wheat corns.

Rose dismounted, deliberately keeping the side of her face with the birthmark turned toward Margrethe. It was as if she were saying, "You might as well see the worst of me." Her blue eyes were waxy and almost defiant. Margrethe smiled in welcome and led the way into the hut. William was beginning to become alert for the evening. He blinked at Rose, who flinched in fear. Margrethe laughed. "Don't worry about William, he is just an ordinary owl. I cared for him when his wing was broken, and now he regards this hut as his home. He is useful. He kills any mice which come in."

Both women were near the same height, but Rose was of a more stocky build. Her hair may have been dark blonde or light brown. It was difficult to tell, for it had never been washed. Rose wore it in an untidy plait that was seldom combed and rebraided. Her gown bore ample evidence of her kitchen work, being spotted with various types of food, stained in splotches, scorched on one sleeve and generally soiled. The riding cloak she wore had been loaned to her by Karyl. Her shoes had been discarded by some larger person. They were much too large but still whole and serviceable.

Margrethe led Rose to a row of pegs set high in the wall. "Here you may hang your garments," she said. She was taken aback when Rose replied, "I be the peg where my gown hangs, lady, and I've naught else."

Margrethe went outside to have a private word with Karyl. "Can you bring woolen cloth when you come again, please? And needles and thread? That girl must have another garment. And perhaps you could bring a comb for me? I tried carving one but my skill was not enough. See?" She hold out a poorly formed comb with half the coarse teeth missing or broken.

Karyl examined it, saying, "You cut the wrong way for the grain in the wood. That's why the tooth broke easily. I will bring you one of Berta's combs."

"Although I dislike asking for so much when you have already been so kind, could you also bring me Berta's old spindles and some wool? There is so little to occupy the time here. I could spin some fine wool yarn from which any number of things could be made."

Karyl agreed, then said, "Let me show Rose where to fetch the water while it is yet day. Then I will be gone." Rose came obediently when Karyl called, brought the pail and set off cheerfully with Karyl.

Margrethe breathed a quick prayer, "Dear Jesu and holy Augustine who first brought the faith to this place, I rejoice and give thanks to have this new companion for my life. Bless thou my protector Karyl. May he be strengthened. Forgive my sin. Amen."

William had decided that the time was right for his hunting to begin. Margrethe opened the door for him, and he sailed out as Karyl and Rose returned with the water. Margrethe requested that some water be poured into the large tripod pot on the hearth. Karyl took his leave and the women were alone.

"What would you that I do?" asked Rose

"First lift a bowl of water from the cauldron on the hearth and pour it into the large trencher. Now come and let us lave our hands."

"Why, lady? We have no mud or dung on them."

"The dirt of this day is on them, and I do not choose to eat that dirt."

When they had rubbed their hands in the warm water until the hands were cleaner, Margrethe requested, "Now show me how to use this quern."

Thus did Margrethe begin her initiation into the mysteries of kitchencraft.

From Dorchester to Searisbyrig King Alfred's cavalcade proceeded as soon as the roads were usable after the storm. King Alfred wanted to inspect the repairs of the fortifications at Searisbyrig, which he had ordered.

Edward was as full of questions as ever. "Why is this place encircled by such a funny round mound? Were the people here trying to build a moat?"

"No, Edward, the place has this shape because those who built it were afraid," answered Padraik. "When the Roman conquerors came here more than a thousand years ago they were much feared by the natives. These natives came up here to the top of this hill to live so that they could see enemies approaching from any direction. They made that high dike of dirt to hide their cattle and came out of those narrow openings to fight the Romans."

"Were the Romans bad men?"

"Very bad. They wanted to own the whole world."

"Why?"

"Better ask your grandfather. He owns all this part of the world now."

"Where did all the Romans go?"

"Back to their own land. Back to Rome."

"Were the people here glad when the Romans went home?"

"Some were. Some were not. Edward, you are too young to really understand, but people need a firm government, like your pony needs a firm hand on his reins. If the pony were allowed to run without guidance he would not be much use to you, or to himself. When the Romans left, every little tribe and sometimes even the families within a tribe began to fight with one another. Rulers were killed or conquered so often that the people knew not which direction to go. Every man was afraid of his neighbor, and they all behaved like beasts. Fighting was constant."

"Our people were like that?" asked Edward

"No, not ours. We Saxons came from across the seas on the mainland of Europa. From a place called Saxony. With us we brought order, stability, civilization, progress."

Edward's attention now strayed to his grandfather. "Why is my grandsire looking at that building place?"

"That is where a church is being built to your grandsire's design. He directed our return home from Dorchester in this direction primarily to inspect this new building as well as the repairs to the fortification."

"Is there much danger of attack here now?"

"Not much. But if the Norsemen knew it to be weak, they might come raiding, When the Norse raiders come, our people light signal fires on the hilltops to warn of the danger."

"Padraik, did you ever see any Norsemen?"

"Indeed, yes. They were the traders, though, and not the warriors. In my travels I have met many of them."

Edward looked thoughtful.

"What thinkest thou, child?" asked Padraik.

"My mother used to say to me 'Edward, the world is a marvel.' 'Tis true. And so big!"

At this time the boy was less than twenty leagues from his home. There was yet a journey of another ten leagues before he would reach Winchester, where his grandfather's court was wintering.

A cloud of gloom had descended on Torr Castle. As Helene drew near to time for the delivery of her child, her temper grew short. She was cross with Ethelred, which angered him so that he became unreasonably harsh with his servants, who beat their underlings, who scolded their wives, who mistreated their children, who threw stones at the dogs and kicked the fowls. Thus the whole castle was in a continuous uproar. The only time that a near-harmony prevailed was during the wine drinking after the evening meal.

Helene demanded six maids-in-waiting and, for the sake of peace, got them. She demanded that a wet nurse be found and brought to the castle in readiness for her infant's arrival. It seemed to Ethelred that Helene spent all of her time thinking up new and often unreasonable demands.

Ethelred began to dread meeting Helene each morn. Her time was imminent, and two midwives were moved into the chambers adjoining hers. Less than four weeks after her wedding, Helene went into labor. She shrieked and groaned, sighed, cried, and yelled at every slightest pang. Before her labor had advanced to the second stage, the entire staff of the castle was tired of her noisemaking.

"Foxes have kits, bitches have pups, fowl lay eggs, swine do calve, and horses foal all without such hellish noise," grumbled Ethelred. "We think this a good day to go hunting." The thought cheered him immensely. "While the queen is a-bearing, the king shall go a-bearing." He laughed at his own wit and ordered that the hunt be organized.

The men who rode with Ethelred were happy to be away from the castle. Even chill wind and drizzle were better than enduring Helene's noise. They rode into the woods, the tall trees giving them shelter from the worst of the wind. Sacks of ale and of wine hung from their saddles. In the cold air they had frequent recourse to these sacks for warmth. Better humor was restored to them all. They rode back to the castle after a day spent in the open air without having killed any game.

Ethelred went to inquire of the midwives if his child had been born. "The queen rests now, your majesty, when she awakens the hard labor will begin," was their answer.

Ethelred left quickly, desiring to be out of earshot before Helene awakened. His evening meal was waiting. He gorged himself on food and wine, anticipating a call at any moment from the midwives to come see his new son. He waited until midnight, then all went to bed.

Ethelred slept heavily. He was awakened at first light by a panting servitor who had run up the stairs to bring the news. "A son! Your majesty has another son!" Ethelred dressed quickly and hastened to see the new infant. The boy was wrapped tightly in his swaddling bands. All Ethelred could see of him was a fat red face, eyes tight shut against the light, mouth open to voice protest.

"Is he not beautiful, my husband?" asked Helene.

Ethelred thought not, and would have said as much except that he saw how haggard Helene looked, quite as if she had spent a day on the battlefield. Unexpectedly, he kissed her. "Thanks be to you for this, our new son."

✢ ✢ ✢

Margrethe had kept a careful count of the days, using a smooth stick and a bit of charred wood from the fire to mark it. When Saturday had come, Margrethe put the large trencher on the hearth. She filled it with warm water, and proceeded to horrify Rose. Margrethe removed all of her clothing. Beginning with her face, Margrethe bathed herself all over. She finished by standing with her feet in the water while she dried herself on a kerchief. Covering herself with a cloak she stepped from the water and dried her feet. Her skin glowed pink in the firelight. Now she used her bodkin to daintily clean her toe and fingernails. Rose watched, dumbfounded. She restrained herself from speaking until Margrethe unbound her hair and stood combing the snarls from it. "Lady, is what you have done wise?" Rose asked.

"Certes! It does no harm to cleanse the skin once a week."

"But all over?" Rose looked worried. "I was told that water on the body would make women's monthly times very difficult. I would not have you suffer, lady."

"I suffer more if I feel unclean. I like to feel fresh for the Lord's Day." Margrethe worked with her hair until it hung as smoothly as a golden curtain shot through with silver. There had been no silver in it until her recent troubles began. She said, "Had I but some sope-wort, or sope-wood I would wash my hair, also."

Rose's eyes grow round, "In winter, lady? You will die sure."

"Nonsense! Since my childhood I have always washed my hair four times in the year. It is well to remain by the fire until the hair is dry, but it certainly does no harm."

"Lady, I think no woman except the queen could be more careful of her person." Rose repeated, "The queen!" She looked stunned. "You *are* the queen! But they said you had been killed."

"Rose, I beg you to forget the secret you have just discovered. For if it were known that I yet live, my life and that of the good Karyl would be forfeit. I ask in the name of our sweet Jesu, forget that which you know."

CHAPTER 6

The days passed more tolerably for Margrethe now that she had Rose as a companion. Rose could make tasty soups from unlikely ingredients. She knew how to use the quern to grind fine meal for making bread or coarse meal for porridge. Karyl came by the hut as often as he could bringing gifts of freshly killed game. The first time he brought a hare Margrethe was quite sure that she could cope with the skinning and gutting if someone would show her how. Under Rose's tutelage she set her bodkin to the fur of the hare and found that she could not control the churning of her stomach. Rose laughed at her discomfort. She set about expertly cutting around the paws and neck and peeled the pelt from the hare. The inside out pelt she stretched over a willow-withe. "When we have enough of these, lady, you can have fur mitts and slippers," she said. Then she began to disembowel the carcass. When the intestines slipped out Margrethe hastily got as far away as she could before her stomach emptied itself. She could not go back until the retching weakness was past, by which time Rose had the hare ready for the spit.

Karyl had brought Berta's spindle and some raw wool. Attempting to learn to spin left Rose quite frustrated. Her hands were so rough from heavy work that the wool was snagged by the roughness. Margrethe spun a fine wool yarn smooth and free from variations in texture. The yarn spun by Rose was full of surprises, thick, thin, knotty, smooth. After weeks of practice the best that could be said of Rose's spinning was that she had increased her rate of production.

At Torr Castle Helene was planning a large christening for the new prince. She demanded that the bishop of the area come to officiate.

"Didn't have all this fuss when our Edward was christened. Father John was good enough for him," Ethelred grumbled. Helene affected not to hear him.

The new prince was a cross baby, forever screaming. Physically he was thriving, growing plump on the good breastmilk of his wet nurse. Ethelred stayed as far away from the baby as possible.

The bishop could not come to Torr until well after the turn of the year. The first week in March he appeared at the castle with a large, demanding retinue.

At Helene's behest, Ethelred sent out orders that all of the nobles in his kingdom attend the christening. This included Karyl. Karyl arrived at Torr castle to find it dirtier than he had ever known it to be before. The servants were all slipshod, careless in all their work. Karyl went to speak to Father John.

"Have you word, Father, of Prince Edward?"

"Only seven days past. The messenger said that the boy is well and learning much. Poor Edward would feel sorely out of place if he were here now, with all this fuss over the new baby. Edward was my trial, and my delight. I miss him."

"Of King Alfred, what was said?"

"Naught of real import. He is building defenses here and there. Expecting an invasion of the Norsemen."

"Is there reason to expect such?"

"No word of any has been brought here. But with the Norsemen, who knows?"

"Amen to that, Father, who knows?"

Torr Castle was overcrowded with the guests for the christening. If any thought that it was strange to hold a formal christening for an infant whose parents had only been married three months before, none dared so to say.

Helene was known to be easily affronted. To even hint that her behavior had been less than acceptable was to court drastic retaliation. Lands and houses could be appropriated by the Crown for less; honor and even life itself were sometimes forfeit.

The day of the ceremony dawned squally, cold winds pursuing cold rain showers in rapid succession across the sky. Inside, the castle was bright with torches and candles. The castle chapel could in no way accommodate the crowd. The excess had to stand near the doorways where they could see and hear the ceremony.

The bishop, arrayed in his finest robes, dropped sprinkles of holy water on the child as he intoned, "I christen thee Athelstain, in the name of the Father, and of the Son, and of the Holy Spirit." At this, the princeling screamed lustily. He continued to protest until the service had ended. Helene was as glad as everyone else to see the child's nurse carry him away to be fed and changed.

King Ethelred mopped his scarlet brow. His best fur robe was much too warm to wear indoors in March. He said, "Our Edward made no such outcry when he was christened. He smiled at the cleric instead."

To which Helene's replied, "You are always comparing the two boys. Mayhap time has dimmed your remembrances. Certes Edward was not perfect upon all occasions." Ethelred, eager to get to his drinking, forebore to argue.

Edward was now having lessons in Latin, in the use of weapons, and in manners. The latter caused him the most difficulty. It was an unhappy Edward who was learning his first lessons in kingly behavior at the court in Winchester. Edward was treated as a page, and expected to learn to serve others. He stood behind his Uncle William's chair at meals and learned to serve others by being observant of their needs. He was reprimanded should the wine cup become empty without his noticing. Often Edward sought comfort from Padraik. He told his woes to Padraik with tears.

"Why do I have to wait and eat later?" he asked.

"Because the first thing a boy who will be king must learn is how to control himself."

"But why must I serve my uncle William?"

"Your uncle William is well fitted to help you learn the things which you must know. He only finished his fostering training last year."

"Since he knows how, I think it would be well if he stood behind *my* chair! " Edward looked resentful.

"Come, now Edward, you are no infant. Do not be hateful of the lessons which teach you good manners and courtly behavior."

"I would much prefer to learn to play the lute."

"Do well, and smile while you are serving, and I will promise to teach you to play the lute, if your grandsire agrees."

Edward smiled. "I'll go ask him just now."

Padraik watched the child go and felt pity for the lad. He was so vulnerable, having yet to develop a carapace of toughness for protection against the hurts of life.

After the hard winter, spring came with a rush. April brought new leaves and flowerbuds, and the edge was gone from the chill of darkness. William the owl stirred more restlessly each day. He still hunted by night and slept in the hut by day. He began making crooning sounds at Margrethe and seemed frustrated that she could not reply.

Rose said, "Lady, it be time William found a mate. Dame Nature is telling him about springtime but he is yet confused by his youth. He will go from us one day."

Margrethe, too, felt a restlessness. A sense of foreboding. A warning of dangers hidden, unseen, but present danger. Since her physical sight had been damaged

Margrethe had developed a kind of inner sight. Often in the early hours of the morn all of the major events that would occur during a day would flash through her mind in a series of bright pictures. At first Margrethe shared these pictures with Rose, but Rose was plainly fearful when the pictured events came to pass. She would cross herself and say, "It be witchcraft, lady." Gradually Margrethe ceased to speak of what she called her "picturings," but it did not cease. The picturings increased in number and accuracy as the weeks passed. Her dreams during the night were often revelations of future events, also.

One morn in late April, after a night of restless dreams filled with pursuit and fire, Margrethe told Rose to hurry the morning meal. "Today is the day we go to seek the sope-wort. We'll ride my palfrey down the stream a ways. Perhaps where the stream banks are sheltered we can find the sope-wort. If not, it will still be good to be out in the fresh air." William had not returned to the hut. Rose said, "He found himself a girl owl. Now he will be what he should be, a wild owl, and not a half-taxed creature forever frightening me with his 'Hu-hu-hu-hu-huff.'" Margrethe had always found it amusing when William startled Rose.

After their simple meal, Rose and Margrethe got the bridle and saddle secured on the palfrey. The animal was restless, also, and seemed eager for an outing. The early morning air was chill enough that Margrethe went back to fetch her cloak from the hut and brought her second cloak for Rose to wear.

They used an old tree stump for mounting, Margrethe in the saddle with Rose riding pillion, clinging to her waist.

"Rose, it would be much better were you here in the saddle guiding the horse. I cannot see the path at all."

"No, lady, I've never guided a horse. I'll look sharp and be your eyes."

They proceeded slowly with Rose giving directions. "Right now. Left a bit. 'Ware of a great stone in the path." The mare moved easily and willingly toward the stream. The scents of early spring assailed them. Sharp willow, tender young fern trampled by the horse, bursting leaf buds with their gluey odor and texture. The very fragrance of the earth itself, warmed by the sun. The palfrey nickered on reaching the stream and lowered her head for a drink.

"Urge her to cross the stream here," said Rose. "On the far side are some large boulders we can use to dismount." It took a bit of patience to guide the horse exactly right, then the two women slid safely down onto the firm rocks and stepped down to the soft earth, Margrethe held the leading rein of the horse, as Rose lead her.

The noise of the rushing waters of the stream drowned out all other sound. Rose searched along the banks of the stream, selecting various young green leaves for Margrethe to examine. At last Margrethe said of one plant, "This one is a sope-wort. This is bouncing bet. How much is growing here?"

"A quantity, lady. Let me tether the mare to a tree, then you can kneel and see for yourself."

Margrethe was delighted with the size of their find. "This means clean hair! We can wash our wool gowns in bouncing bet also."

They spent a contented few moments picking the dark-green-leafed plants. Rose stood up and sniffed the air.

"Smell you smoke?" she asked Margrethe.

Margrethe stood. "Yes. Can you see what burns?"

"Not from here, lady. Wait you here, I will go and look." Rose walked downstream, then came running back at top speed.

"Lady, lady," she gasped, "Run! We must run!"

"Calm yourself enough to tell me," Margrethe demanded.

"Norsemen. Berserkers. We smelled their boats burning. They have stacked their armor beside a young man who lies bound hand and foot. They are chanting to their pagan god. Soon they'll be coming." Rose grabbed Margrethe by the hands pulling her along. "Hurry, lady, hurry! You know how it will be with us should the berserkers catch us."

Fear swept through Margrethe but her mind did not panic. "Quickly, Rose, get us back to the rocks where we dismounted. Bring the palfrey there." Rose did it. "Now you mount in front, and I'll get up behind. You must guide the horse, and make all speed." Margrethe clapped her heels against the horse's flanks and it broke into a run. Rose, holding the rains in unpracticed hands gave the wrong signals to the horse, but the fear of the women had transmitted itself to the animal and it ran as strongly as possible.

"Guide her on the road to Karyl's manor house. We must give warning," ordered Margrethe.

On the road ahead they came upon a group of peasants who had been gathering faggots. "Berserkers! Berserkers!" screamed Rose and Margrethe. The peasants threw down their bundles of wood and raced for their homes.

The mare was blowing hard before their wild ride was finished. Several people near the manor were working at a leisurely pace until the women came abreast of them crying "Berserkers!" Then panic spread like wildfire.

"Where to now, lady?"

"Find Karyl. We must warn him. Is there a mounting block where we can get down?"

The exhausted mare drooped patiently beside the stone block. The women found that their legs felt very weak as they started up the stone steps of the manor house. Karyl came out the door. "What's amiss?" he called.

"Berserkers! Burned their boats on the stream bank near the hut."

"Lord God be with us! How many?"

"Rose saw two boats burning. Perhaps eighty men. Had a bound captive as a sacrifice victim lying beside their pile of armor."

"Get inside the house quickly," said Karyl. "Rose, you go to the kitchens. You'll be safe there. I want our lady to be in a more secluded place." Karyl led Margrethe up several long stairways to an attic room. He said, "None come here in the course of a day, You will be alone. I must go." He dashed down the stairs, leaving Margrethe railing at the blindness that kept her from seeing what was happening.

It was as well that she could not see. Thick black smoke now boiled up from the hut where she had been living. The contents of the hut were too poor to become loot. The berserkers had set fire to it after drinking up the keg of ale.

Margrethe could hear horns calling the men to assemble to defend the manor house. Karyl dispatched one rider on a swift horse to give warning to Torr Castle.

Karyl paced up and down while waiting for his men to assemble. The men were not warlike and were poorly armed. It was not likely that they could hold the manor against the determined berserkers. Villeins with their livestock were pouring in through the gate to the manor house yard. Karyl directed them to the stables in the rear. More columns of smoke marked the advance of the berserkers.

When most of his men had gathered around him, Karyl asked "Are there four boys here who can climb well?" Half a dozen stepped forward. Karyl chose the four largest. "I want you boys up in those two oak trees which flank the courtyard gate. Each boy is to be supplied with two leather buckets of water. When the berserkers pass beneath you heading for the gates throw the water on their torches. If those torches are doused they won't set fires here. Quickly now, up those trees, boys."

As the four lads scrambled up the oaks, Karyl sent men to fetch the buckets of water. He then assigned four bowmen to hide behind the trunks of the trees where the boys were stationed, "When the boys throw the water you men shoot at the berserkers. They wear no armor. Wherever your arrows hit they will penetrate, I want four more men up on top of that wall. Lie flat until the berserkers pass through this gate. Then stand and fire as rapidly as possible." Men began to boost the archers up to the top of the wall. "Remember to stay hidden," Karyl warned them. "Surprise is to be a weapon for us. Men who have horses here come with me. The rest of you arm yourselves as best you can and take cover. I'll take those other two boys with me to the manor house. They can man the arrow slits which flank the front entrance."

Karyl and the boys raced toward the house, with the horse owners following. Karyl stationed a boy at each arrow slit saying, "Remember that it is up to you to shoot to kill any intruder who comes near this front door. Don't let the shouting of the berserkers frighten you. They are just as mortal as other men." He handed the boys each a bow and a quiver of arrows. "The safety of this house is in your hands."

Karyl and the horsemen then ran to the stables. "If you have battle pads to protect you steeds, use them. If not, saddle up, get your weapons and follow me."

The panic of the men had spread to the horses. They danced and neighed, tossed their heads, stamped and were most difficult to saddle and bridle. Karyl's armorer was busily handing out lances and swords to those who had left their weapons at home. When all had mounted, Karyl led his troop to a position behind the manor, where they would be hidden from the sight of the invading berserkers. "Men, this battle will be fierce," said Karyl, "We fight for our lives and those of our families. We are outnumbered, but we shall win. This is a Christian land, and the forces of Odin and Thor shall not prevail over our Lord Jesu Christos and Jehovah."

Now the hidden men could hear the shouting of the war chants as the berserkers trotted up the road toward the gate. Karyl wished most furiously that he could see what was happening.

The berserkers passed beneath the oak trees where the boys were hidden. The boys threw their buckets of water. Three of the four torches were extinguished. An angry roar went up from the mob, but before they could begin to seek out the boys, a flight of arrows from the rear herded them through the gate. Some were down now, at least five dead and three mortally wounded. The archers hidden atop the wall accounted for seven more before the berserkers ran beyond bow shot.

As the berserkers came yelling across the courtyard, a frightened six-year-old girl broke from her hiding place, calling for her mother. In a few long strides the berserker with the torch grabbed the child and set her long braids alight with his torch. Then he released the screaming, burning, living torch, laughing as she ran wildly trying to escape the pain of the flames.

Her anguished cries brought Karyl and the horsemen out of hiding. The Norsemen stood their ground and fought with fury. They had no chance against trained war steeds mounted by warriors. The men who were mounted on farm horses had their difficulties. These farm horses were disconcerted by the howls of the invaders. The Norsemen, fighting with a broadsword in one hand and a battle ax in the other, slashed and chopped these farm horses, reducing them to bloody carcasses. Karyl seemed to be everywhere at once on his destrier, encouraging, killing, directing, trampling fallen berserkers.

One berserker darted from the group and ran to the rear of the manor house. He found the kitchen door barred and hurled himself repeatedly at the solid oak planking until the hinges gave way and the door fell inward. The women in the kitchen screamed and fled except for Rose. She felt a wave of cold fury sweep over her. With a strength greater than normal she grabbed the heavy iron griddle used for baking cakes and swung it at the invader's head. The point caught him above the right ear and his head burst open, splattering brains and gore over Rose and much of the kitchen. Shaking from sudden weakness brought on by shock, fear, and strain, Rose forced herself to pick up the berserker's sword and battle ax. She went from the kitchen to the main hall, and there collapsed, weeping, as the sound of battle horns was heard.

King Ethelred and his troop had ridden hard as soon as the messenger from Karyl had reached them. Now there was no longer a doubt as to the outcome of the battle.

Outnumbered and surrounded by well-trained armed men, the berserkers still fought on. They fought until the last one was killed, inflicting many injuries during their last moments.

Ethelred's face was flushed with wild joy of battle. He had killed and triumphed over the Norsemen. He laughed and clasped Karyl by the hand as a brother warrior, "Well fought, well fought," he said. "It could be that King Alfred is right to be strengthening his fortifications against these Norsemen."

Karyl was mortally tired by his efforts of the morning, but he thought this was a right time to make a request. "Your majesty, could you grant permission for me to castellate the manor house? I would like to be better prepared should the raiders come again."

"Why not? We so grant it. We may not always be within our walls when you next need aid. We do not wish to lose so valiant a warrior. Castellate. It will give our kingdom more power against such as these." Ethelred smiled happily.

"I thank your majesty." Karyl left the king and went to give orders to his people regarding the disposition of the dead berserkers. He ordered a huge pit be dug as a mass grave. The weapons were to be collected and stored in his armory. There were dead men among his own to account for, as well as many wounded men to be taken to the infirmary. The results of the battle could have been worse. After the villeins had fled to the manor house yard for protection, no woman had been injured or killed. Among the children, only the little girl who had been set aflame was dead. One of the boys who had been in the oak trees at the gate had fallen from the tree and had broken a leg. The excited boys who had manned the arrow slits came to report to Karyl.

"We did as you said. We guarded the front door. One Norseman ran up to the steps, and I shot him."

"No, I shot him!"

"It was my arrow went through his neck. He was down on the ground then, flopping around like a fowl with a wrung neck for a long time before he died."

"Good lads. Now go help the men with the burial pit." Karyl smiled at the boys as he entered his house. In the great hall he found a knot of women gathered around Rose, who was weeping piteously. Karyl hastened over to them. He could see that Rose was splattered with gore and brains.

"Are you hurt, girl?"

Rose gulped, tried to speak, and shook her head. She pointed to the kitchen. Karyl went to look, and was amazed to find the dead berserker. He returned to Rose.

"You killed him?" Karyl asked.

Rose nodded, and handed the battle ax and the sword to Karyl. He gave them to one of the women to be taken to the armory.

"Come with me, Rose." Karyl took her by the hand and pulled her to her feet. She trembled when walking, and he steadied her with an arm about her waist as he led her up the stairs to the attic room where Margrethe was hidden.

"I'll be back soon with water and food. See if you can quiet Rose. She isn't injured." Karyl left.

Margrethe seated Rose on the bed. She sat beside her and held her hand. Soon Rose began to speak. "Oh, lady, it was horrid. The Norseman came at me, and I hit him with the griddle and killed him. This mess all over me is his blood and his brains. Lady, I'm sorry I laughed when you were sickened by the gutting of the hare. When this berserker's head burst open, I knew how you felt. I did worse than you, I just vomited right there on the kitchen floor."

Margrethe said, "Let's get this gown off you."

"But I've nothing to put on."

"We can wrap my cloak around you." She helped Rose remove the soiled gown and wrapped the cloak around her.

Karyl returned with the food and water. Addressing Margrethe he said, "King Ethelred is staying in the house. You will have to remain here in this room and keep quiet until he goes tomorrow. We would not have won this day without the aid of him and his fighting men. I must at least give them one night of hospitality." He left, and the women were alone. Rose lay down on the bed when Margrethe ordered her to do so. But she protested when Margrethe poured some of the water on a napkin and began bathing her face. "Lady, it is not right that you should cleanse me."

"Why not? By your action you may have saved all of the women in this house. Surely it is little enough to do for you to wipe your face clean. Now your hair is really in need of washing. Can you wipe the spots from your own hands and arms?"

Rose did her best, after which Margrethe poured more water on the napkin and tried to remove the spots from Rose's hair. Unfortunately most of then were already dry and they resisted removal. As she worked, Margrethe's sense of humor came bubbling up. She could not restrain it. Rose looked surprised when Margrethe giggled, "Rose, Rose. Just yesterday I was thinking how much we were in need of the sope-wort. Little did I dream how much more in need of it we would be on this day."

CHAPTER 7

The captive of the berserkers, who had been left beside their stack of armor when they had gone raiding, was taken to Karyl's manor house along with the armor. This captive was thin and soiled and found to have a severely injured leg. Karyl ordered him taken to the infirmary along with the wounded. When given food, the lad ate ravenously, while surrounding his bowl with his arms as if fearful that it might suddenly be snatched from him. He slept fitfully, and uttered strange cries, which disturbed the other patients in the infirmary. What language he spoke they knew not. It clearly was not English, nor did it sound like the tongue of the Norsemen.

The next day, following the departure of King Ethelred and his fighters, Karyl went to discuss the captive with Margrethe.

"A pity it is that we don't have Padraik here," she said. "In his travels he has learnt so many tongues that he might recognize what this young man speaks."

"The other injured in the infirmary complain of the noises this lad makes. He is in need of care, but he does disturb everyone with his outcries. Would you take him here to care for?" asked Karyl.

"Not unless you can find another gown for Rose. All she has to wear is my old cloak, and it has no fastenings to preserve her modesty. We would also have to get more food and water, as well as another bed."

"I shall see that you get all you require. In a few days I will get you removed to another place. I know of a house on the edge of a village, deep in the forest, five leagues from here."

"Thanks be to you, Karyl, for all of your aid to me. Caring for the injured lad will be little enough to repay you. You are kind to think of my comfort when you have so much to do."

"My lady, I am pledged to ever protect and honor you. I keep my pledges." With this, Karyl was gone. He returned in a short time with several servitors bearing the bed, three gowns, food, a huge vessel of water, salves, bandages, and the wounded captive.

The boy could not have been more than seventeen. He had the fuzzy beginnings of a beard. His hands and feet seemed too large for his frame, as if his full growth had yet to be reached. Pale blue eyes glanced quickly at the women and away again, as if he did not want to be discovered staring at them. His hair was nearly as red as Rose's firebrand birthmark.

Rose joined willingly in aiding Margrethe to care for the boy. Together they washed him, tended his wound, fed him, and spoke softly to him and smiled often. The second day after being brought under their care the lad responded with a timid smile. "Tammas," he said, pointing to himself. "Tammas." Now they had a name for him.

"Tammas. But Tammas the what? That is our puzzle," said Margrethe.

To which Rose replied, "Lady, if his leg heals, and he do walk again, we will likely call him Tammas the Lame."

Ethelred had sent word by a royal courier to the court of King Alfred at Winchester regarding the raid by the berserkers. Edward overheard the message of the couriers and went running to find Padraik.

"Padraik, Padraik, heard you the news?" the child's eyes grew large with excitement.

"What news?"

"About the Norsemen. The berserker raiders. They did come, and my sire, he fought them and killed them!"

"He did this all alone?"

"Well, he does have some fighting men to help him, you know."

"Did the Norsemen attack Torr Castle?"

"No. I think the raid was on the fief of Karyl's, that knight who used to help my mother."

Padraik blanched with fear for the safety of his well-loved Margrethe. "What also do you know of this raid?"

"Naught. I only heard the courier tell my grandsire that much."

Padraik went to speak to the courier. He found him to be boorish and of limited intelligence. The courier had only a secondary knowledge of the raid, he not being a fighting man.

"Were many killed by the berserkers?" asked Padraik

"Some. Mostly villeins. Some of the men serving the knight Karyl."

"Women, too?"

"Mayhap. I wist not. You know that Norsemen kill any and all without difference."

This conversation did nothing to calm Padraik's concern about Margrethe. Naught he could do about that now but pray.

After getting the news of the raid, King Alfred decided to investigate the condition of the fortifications of his port cities. He had intended to move his court nearer to the seashore for the summer but, in view of this raid, decided against it. He traveled with a very small retinue to see if changes should be made in the coastal fortifications ranging from Pevensey to Porchester. Porchester was the largest of these shore forts that had been built up in past centuries to repel the invading Saxons. Now the Saxons were using them to defend against other invaders.

While King Alfred was away on his defensive work, Padraik began the long-promised lute lessons for Edward. Edward's eagerness to play the lute soon dimmed.

"Why no practicing?" asked Padraik.

"The lute strings cut my fingers," replied Edward, showing his soft fingertips grooved and bruised from the lute strings.

"That is because your fingers are not properly callused."

"How can I get the calluses?"

"Just by continuing to practice even though your fingertips do ache from it."

Edward tried again. Padraik found him later sobbing in a corner. "Oh Padraik, why are things which look so pleasant so hard and painful?"

"Lad, you have just discovered one of the great riddles of this world. No one has the answer to that. We must just keep trying until the hard things become easy. You will play well in time, but practice you must."

"Think I'd rather just have you play. You can do it good. You have plenty of calluses."

"That would be well enough for now. But what will happen when you grow to be a young man and desire to court a lady for the Maying? I cannot play for you then, or sing the ballads you would use to woo your damsel."

"Padraik, why must I always suffer now so I will be better later? Why don't we start out in life already better and not have to drudge at it?"

"Only the Lord God knows the answer to that, child."

Torr Castle was soon disturbed again by news of the Norsemen. On the return trip from Winchester, the courier had seen three boatloads of Norsemen approaching the mouth of the Stour. Until this, the courier had been dawdling on his return, enjoying riding through the young spring. Now with a fresh force of Norsemen at hand, he made all speed to report to Ethelred. The courier's horse was well-nigh dead from haste when they reached Torr Castle.

Ethelred received the news calmly. "Where were these Norsemen going?" he asked.

"Your majesty, from the sea they had come into the estuary, heading into the Stour mouth. When I saw that I hastened to bring you word. Where they were going, and where they are now, I cannot say."

"What they are, we know well. They are troubles sent by the devil to plague us. They make good hunting sport, though. We dismiss you to your food and rest."

Ethelred sat and plotted his actions. The Norsemen should make a few days sport, hunting and fighting. Only three boatloads he could handle easily with the troops in the castle. Better to start now, though, before the invaders moved too far inland. He strode toward his armory calling to his trumpeters, "Sound the alarm. Sound the alarm. We go to hunt the Norsemen." The blaring trumpets awakened the little prince Athelstain. His screams of protest gave Ethelred another reason to hasten away.

King Ethelred and his warriors rode forth from the castle in full war regalia. The horses wore thick pads against injury to their chests and bodies. The men wore heavy leather armors connected by sections of chainmail at the joints. They were all well armed with swords and lances. Some carried maces, and a few, including the king, had the deadly new weapon, the morningstar. This was a refined development from the mace, using the same type of spiked iron ball and sturdy handle, but having the ball mounted on a heavy iron chain so that it could be swung to gain greater impact power. Properly wielded it could destroy any opponent. Morningstars could be used equally well on horseback or on foot. The mere sight of a platoon armed with morningstars was often enough to cause the surrender of enemy armies.

They had fewer than eight leagues to ride to the Stour mouth, yet it was too far to reach by twilight. An encampment was made for the night, and they set forth fresh the next morn.

They searched the banks of the Stour up and down, and found a few burned-out huts and murdered people, but no Norsemen. There was a plainly marked area where the boats had been dragged up onto the sand and a fire had been built. They must have been here overnight but now were gone. They had evidently gone back to the sea in their boats. Ethelred and the men spent several days searching for these Norsemen. To no avail. The Norsemen may have put into the Stour just to replenish their supplies of food and water. Whatever their purpose Ethelred mistrusted it. If three Norse boats could put in without hindrance, then a much larger fleet could do the same. Ethelred dispatched another courier to inform King Alfred.

Karyl was kept busy designing the castellation of his manor. There were to be round towers, one at each corner of the building, with strong battlements. He had ordered that temporary shelters be set up inside the manor courtyard. These were to be used by the homeless villeins whose help he needed during the construction work. Not being skilled in stone masonry, these villeins had to be taught their tasks slowly. Karyl often became impatient with their lack of speed but found that any show of annoyance on his part only confused and upset the laborers and impeded their progress even more.

Meanwhile, Tammas was improving daily under the care of Margrethe and Rose. One of the gowns that Karyl had brought was bright blue in color. Tammas showed much interest in it. He spoke to the women in his own tongue, but to them it was as the chatter of the daws. He reached out for the gown, and when Margrethe held it near him, he mimed painting his face with the blue cloth.

"Well, now we know," said Margrethe. "Tammas is a Pict. They paint their faces blue."

"A Pict, lady?"

"Yes. Long centuries ago the Picts lived here where we do, but the Roman soldiers drove them northward. The

Picts continued to move north and now live up among the wild Scots. Tammas must have been captured on the far northern coast by the berserkers. My sire said that what they speak is called 'Pictish.' No other peoples speak such a tongue. It is unlike all other language."

Tammas listened intently as if determined to understand. Margrethe smiled at him. "Poor lad, none to speak with in your own tongue. In a year or two you will speak English, mayhap in less time than that."

Tammas could only smile in reply.

Karyl had not forgotten his plan to move the women to a safer location. One of the four villages on his fief was Swinstig, set in the midst of thick groves of oaks. Swine had been raised here from early centuries, growing fat on the good acorn maste, hence the name Swinstig. On the edge of the village was a cottage of wattle-and-daub construction, well-thatched. It had a large room and a kitchen below and sleeping rooms above.

Rose exclaimed in delight to find that so grand a house was to be their residence, "Lady, do you but look! A window with real glass in it."

The uneven-textured diamond panes of glass were set into lead and framed to fit a small window. One could not see through it without great distortions, but it did admit much light.

"My trusted bailiff dwelt here," explained Karyl. "He died but recently of great age. No one has lived here since. Such furnishings as there are must do for you until such time as I complete the fortifications on the manor."

Rose asked, "Have we leave to grow fowls here? I see much space for a hen yard and a garden. With Tammas to help we could grow food in plenty."

"Have what you will," replied Karyl. "All that I have will ever belong to my lady." He gave them a small bag of gold coins to purchase necessities and departed.

Rose was well content. "This is better by far than where we did live, lady. This house can be home."

CHAPTER 8

Swinstig proved to be fair in which to live. The other inhabitants of the hamlet were too busy with their own affairs to bother with the new occupants of the cottage. The cottage became more comfortable each day as Rose and Margrethe worked in it. When a proper knife was purchased for him from a peddler, Tammas showed good skill in carving. Wooden spoons and spatulas, a trencher for kneading dough, flat plates, and other wooden items he created easily. He often saw the need for an item and began making it before the women were aware of their lack.

Rose had plans to set Tammas to delving in the garden as soon as his leg healed. This did not meet with his approval. His few words of English did not permit him a free expression of his feelings on the matter, but his looks and attitude made it plain that he felt such labor beneath him. Only if Margrethe herself took spade in hand would Tammas say, "No lady, no," and push her gently aside. Then he worked, but no harder than necessary unless Rose were watching.

Tammas did help build the hen yard, fencing it and making a house for the fowl. The fowls seemed to approve his labor. Several of the hens became broody and nested, producing a dozen chicks each. This gave promise of a steady supply of eggs as well as an occasional fowl for the table. The young cockerels sang their imperfect screechy greetings to the dawn each morn. "Sing away," Rose cried to them. "The louder the song, the sooner the pot."

The days passed quickly into weeks. Summer seemed too short a time to prepare for the winter. There was wood to gather, fruit and wild berries to dry, the garden produce to tend. A nearby streamlet ran into the Stour farther down its course. This streamlet Tammas would fish, sometimes being rewarded with a catch. Had he been able to walk any great distance he would have caught more fish. But it was as Rose had predicted—his leg wound left him lame.

Margrethe had procured more wool and spindles and a loom. The summer days did not admit of much time for spinning and weaving. Winter would be the season for that.

October brought hard frosts, and the time for nutting. There were walnuts and burr nuts to be gathered in the woods. Rose provided guidance; the three went into the woods for the nuts. Tammas carried a stout stave which was well. He used it to help himself along, but on this nutting trip he needed it for another reason. They were walking peacefully, enjoying the crunchings of the dried leaves underfoot the far-off tang of wood smoke, and the sight of the scarlet, autumn-touched vines. Suddenly they were startled by the rush of an animal, which knocked Rose off her feet. She screamed, and the creature turned back on them savagely. It was a large rogue boar pig. Tammas whacked at it with his stave and shouted loudly. This pig must have once been part of a tame herd, for he seemed to know that the stave was a weapon to be respected. He backed off, snorting, squealed a challenge, and made another rush. Tammas met the attack firmly, and the boar trotted off. They could hear him crashing through the thicket as he went.

The attack had left Rose white and shaking. "Lady, should we come this way again let us all carry staves. When I was young and living in my home village I saw a small child eaten by boars. It was still alive and screaming as the boars ripped into it, I had bad dreams for years after of boars attacking and being unable to run."

Margrethe had carried a slender rod to help her find her way, but it would not have been of any use against the boar. She said, "I fear me that I would make but a poor defense against an enemy which I could not see at all." What Margrethe would not express aloud was her growing certainty that her already limited vision was fading even more. When she missed the beaker when pouring ale and the liquid spilled on the floor or when she failed to set a bowl far enough onto the table and the bowl fell off the edge, she would try to laugh as if it did not matter. "I've grown to have the ways of a cloddish clown," she would say.

✣ ✣ ✣

As the autumn deepened into winter, Padraik went on a mission for King Alfred. When he returned he brought a gift for Edward—a lute of his own. It lay in its case, golden and enticing until Padraik had time to string it and set the pegs properly. As Padraik worked on the lute Edward chattered. "Oh Padraik, I love the beauty of it." Edward ran his fingertips over the smooth surface. "It feels like music."

"More so than my lute?"

"Yes. This is the singer that I can teach to sing my songs. Your lute is full of your music."

"Then teach it well. You will get to take it with you when we go to visit your father."

"We are going to Torr Castle? How soon?"

"King Alfred said we are to go in January. You will have been with us for a year then, and it will be well for you to see your old home."

"My sire will take me to hunt. I know he will. And he will be astounded at how well I can shoot my arrows now." Edward was delighted, then a cloudy thought came to diminish his sunshine. "Padraik, think you that my sire could love the new prince more than me?"

"Never. Edward, you are the true-born first son, and the rightful heir to the throne."

"How long now before we go?"

"Do you know how long a fortnight is?"
"Yes. That is fourteen days."
"Three fortnights must pass before we go."
"A very long time." Edward drooped.

Padraik placed the newly strung lute into Edward's hands and said, "The time will just be long enough for you to work your music into this."

Edward smiled a secretive cunning smile.

"What a pity," thought Padraik, "the lad has so much of his sire in him. Mayhap this fosterage could modify Edward's heritage. Mayhap not."

Winter carpeted the hills and vales with snow. The copse on the hilltops stood out in stark contrast to the white. But this was not the harsh winter of the preceding year. It was cold, reasonably so. Cold enough to thicken the pelts on the wild game. Not cold enough to keep men indoors.

King Ethelred had demanded from his subjects their full share of enforced labor on the king's roads before the winter began. These main thoroughfares were now in good repair. Frequent travel kept the roads open, some nobles even were complaining that the roads were over traveled with not enough build-up of snow on them to make travel easy for the sledges.

The courier sent by King Alfred to Torr Castle had no trouble with the road as he traveled. Upon his arrival he met the usual resistance to easy admittance at the main gate and at the door to the great hall. At long last the man came to stand before Ethelred. The courier gladly relinquished the parchment scroll he had carried protectively.

Father John, the cleric, unrolled the scroll and studied it carefully, slowly deciphering each word before he read out the message to his king.

> To Ethelred, King of Wessex, from Alfred, King of Sussex. Know you that we will pay to your court a visit in the month of January, bringing with us your noble son. Our court will be with us. We do much desire to see your defenses built against the Norsemen.
>
> *Alfred Rex*
> *His seal*

Ethelred glowed with pleasure, "Our son Edward comes to visit us! That is well, that is very well. What say you Helene?"

To which Helene replied, "Well, indeed, my husband. Let us hope that the boy has learned manners and that his noisy ways do not disturb our son."

Little Prince Athelstain still spent nine-tenth of his waking time in screaming. The remaining one-tenth he spent eating. He was round as a ball of cheese and made no effort yet to either walk or talk. The noise he made always brought what he desired. Few other noises ever seemed to penetrate his consciousness.

The castle cooks were set to baking. The huntsmen brought in more game than normal, which would be smoked, dried, or frozen to provide for Alfred's army of retainers.

The castle halls were littered with old refuse and cobwebs draped the corners and hung from the beams. "Order up a general castle cleaning," Ethelred commanded Helene. "We never had such a sty to live in when Margrethe was our queen. You would shame us before our brother kings with your slovenly ways!"

"Beat the servants then, for their want of diligence. A queen does not work."

"The work of the queen is to see that inside the castle all things are done well and that there is order in the household."

"I please you not?"

"Not when you fail your duty."

"I gave you a son."

"That was lust, we think, and not from love. If love you have for us, then make our castle bright and fresh as it should be."

Helene had the servants beaten, which stirred their resentment against her. They slowed their work pace until she screamed and ranted against them.

Ethelred heard her ravings and said, "How is it you cannot manage these underlings without abuse? A beaten dog never hunts willingly."

To this Helene made no reply. She glared at Ethelred with hate-filled eyes.

The days of Christmas were on them. Father John still lamented the loss of Edward as his altar boy. The Christmas mass was not well attended, the court taking their direction from the behavior of the queen.

This year Helene, too, rode out on the Christmas hunt. The ride was long and tiring, but Helene's joy blazed up when she saw the helpless wounded beasts slaughtered. It was a fierce delight to see the blood gush from the severed throats of the huntsmen's victims. A prime stag was wounded, and run until he fell. He raised his head and looked with shining, frightened eyes at his killers. Helene was in at his death. She laughed aloud as the glow of life left the stag's eyes and his proud head dropped to earth.

The confining cold of January was a time of learning for Tammas and Rose. Margrethe spent much time teaching both of them. Tammas she taught patiently, a few new words each day. Rose was learning to set the web and weave on the loom.

The winter light came but dimly through the small glass window for only about six hours of the day. Rose and Margrethe augmented this light with candles of their own manufacture. Tallow, of course, as they had no wax.

Throwing the shuttle and banging the treadle with its monotonous thump, thump, made a musical rhythm in the cottage. Either Rose or Margrethe worked at the loom almost all of the day. Even so, the cloth grew slowly. Rose had not the speed of Margrethe and was often discouraged. If she said aught about it, Margrethe would set her to spin, which she disliked.

Tammas spent much of his time whittling wood. He made useful items, which seemed like luxuries to the two women who had done without so many things the previous winter. On occasion he found a bit of wood that really pleased him, then he would carve it into an animal. His eye for form was true, and the shape of his half-finished carvings gave the line impressions of the finished item. Tammas carved a whimsical fat bear licking its paw, a doe with her fawn, a flying kestrel.

One day Tammas pulled a stick of charcoal from the hearth and found a flat board. He drew crude stick figures, a large man and woman, holding the hands of five children. One of the children he marked with an X. This picture Tammas took to show Margrethe. He said, "Me, Tammas," pointing to the child marked with the X. Then pointing to the other figures, "Mine fadder, modder . . ." He grew exasperated not knowing the words for brother and sister. Margrethe pointed questioningly, "Brothers? Sisters?" Tammas just shook his head. Margrethe pointed to herself and Rose, "Girls," then to Tammas, "Boy." "Girls, sisters. Boys, brothers," she explained.

Enlightenment replacing his frustration Tammas pointed to one child figure. "Boy—brudder." He pointed to the other three, "Girl—sister."

Turning the flat board over, Tammas sketched busily. He drew a dragon ship and stick warriors with weapons and shields. In this picture the father mother and four children figures were lying flat, while one child was being led away with a rope around his neck. "Tammas." Pointing to the family figures he said, "Dead."

Margrethe was all warm sympathy, "Poor Tammas, no family left. Rose can be your sister."

"Not me, lady. Family I don't need. Family gave me naught but kicks and curses. I wish mine was dead!" Rose protested.

"Rose, we must not death-wish anyone."

"Not even those berserkers?"

"Our Lord says not."

"Never heard Him say aught, myself."

The sky was heavily overcast when the court of King Alfred arrived at Torr Castle. King Ethelred came out to greet them before they had dismounted at the stables. That tall boy, who sat his mount so well, was that Edward?

At that moment Edward saw his father. "Sire, sire," he called excitedly. "Good it is to see you." He jumped into his father's upraised arms.

Ethelred laughed and said, "Come. Come quickly into the castle."

Edward held back. "First I must tend and groom my pony."

"Nonsense! Such as that is for the stable boys. You are my first-born son and prince of this realm."

Edward looked questioningly at King Alfred, who nodded. The two kings together, with Edward leading the way, went up to the great hall of the castle.

Edward was highly pleased to be the center of attention from all the residents of Torr Castle. The household was in an uproar over him.

Father John came scurrying, calling, "Edward, my own lad." Edward could not resist displaying his new learning by greeting the cleric in Latin. "Do but hear the boy," said the cleric, "Good Latin and him so young."

"I have a tutor," said Edward. "He is not easy to please. Glad I am that he stayed in Winchester. I have no desire to spoil this home visit with studies."

Edward's good manners and ready smile charmed the court of his father. They had all quite forgotten what a delight it could be to have a child in their midst. After all, little Athelstain was no joy to anyone.

At table that evening Edward conversed brightly with those seated near him. He paid compliments to Helene and signaled the wine steward when her cup wanted refilling.

When Ethelred had settled to his after dinner wine and walnuts, Edward asked, "Sire, would it please you to have music?"

"Mayhap," replied Ethelred, "what music had you in mind?"

"Music of my own making. I now have a lute." Edward sent a servitor to fetch the lute. Edward tested the strings, tightened a peg or two. Deliberately not looking at Padraik, Edward announced, "I will give you now the 'Fly Song.'" Padraik looked stunned as Edward began.

> *There was a little fly*
> *And he flew in the castle hall*
> *He went* fftt *upon the ceiling,*
> *He went* fftt *upon the wall.*
> *He flew into the kitchen*
> *For to test the cook's jam*
> *He went* fftt *upon the cheeses*
> *He went* fftt *upon the ham.*
> *This fly flew in the chamber*
> *Where the cleric was in bed*
> *The little fly went* fftt fftt fftt,
> *Upon his tonsured head.*

The wine steward was passing Padraik, who put out a foot and tripped the man. The wine he carried splashed over Helene, whose angry screechings ended Edward's concert. Helene and her ladies left the table.

Ethelred turned to Edward with open arms. "That was well done child. We liked that song. It pleased us much. Was that all of the song which you sang?"

"No, sire, but let us wait until another day to have it all. Now, please, have I leave to retire? The day has been long."

"We shall all retire. Come, come." Ethelred clapped his hands, "Cover the fire, all retire."

The company rose from the table, and the servitors began to clear away. Edward and Padraik headed up the stairs to Edward's old room.

"Why did you disgrace my teachings?" asked Padraik.

"I did not."

"With that 'Fly Song' you did!"

"Well, my sire liked that song. You never taught me any song he would like."

"Boy, you have much to learn about what is proper music for a court after they have dined. Where did you learn that disgraceful song?"

"From the stable boys at Winchester."

"The songs of stable boys are not proper in the castle hall."

"But my sire liked it, anyway."

To this Padraik could only reply, "Go to bed, boy, and move over. I share your bed whilst we are here."

Early in the morn King Alfred approached Ethelred. "Did you not tell us that the knight Karyl had been given leave to castellate his manor after the attack by the Vikings?"

"That is so."

"We would like to ride this day to inspect his defenses. Have you an objection?"

"None. This day a hunt has been planned for Edward, and we would not disappoint the lad. Would you go without us?"

"Is there a guide who can lead us to the fief of this Karyl?"

"We shall send the best one with you."

Ethelred was good as his word. A stolid heavy-set man who knew the country well was assigned the task of guide. King Alfred elected to ride out with only two men at arms to accompany him. It was a ride of nearly three hours before they reached Karyl's manor.

Karyl was surprised by the royal visit. King Alfred sent his men at arms along with the guide to find refreshment for themselves among Karyl's servitors.

"Now, Karyl, we would to see our daughter."

"Is that wise, your majesty? Should a king be seen going into the cottage the villeins may suspect who the lady really is."

"Then we will go as a common man. Get us clothing and a plain horse. My destrier, Great John, is too grand for a common man to own."

Karyl fetched the clothing himself, smiling to see that without his royal robes a king was very like any other man. Seated on a farm pony, Alfred still rode like a king.

"Stoop a bit, your majesty. Let your shoulders and back sag. Sit like a half-filled bag of meal." Alfred did his best, but would automatically pull his shoulders straight and his back erect so that Karyl had to remind him often of the role he was playing.

"We are grateful to you for preserving the life of our daughter. We recognize the peril to yourself."

"She is my lady, and I am pledged to her service, your majesty. I will ever care for her."

They arrived at the cottage and rapped at the door. Rose opened to see Karyl and a strange man. Karyl asked, "Rose, can you take Tammas and stay in the kitchen for a time? I will join you shortly. Don't question, girl, this is important."

Rose led Tammas into the kitchen as Alfred entered the large room. His daughter was seated at the loom. He walked up to her.

"Margrethe?"

"Father?" She stood and held out her hands. "My father, here?" He moved within reach of her hands. Tears poured down her face as she leaned her head against his chest. "Oh Father, my heart did so desire to see you again."

Margrethe led him to a settle beside the hearth. "Tell me of my son?"

"Edward is well. Growing and learning. A bright lad. We've brought him to visit his father. Padraik has taught him to play the lute. He is headstrong, but will be a credit to his throne, if it be that he has one. How is it with you, daughter?"

"As well as it can be with one whose own wedded husband has sought her death and by whose schemes she is near blinded. Tell me, Father, are my eyes still red-rimmed from the poison?"

"No. They look not red, but clouded. You can see but little?"

"Yes. And of late, that little grows even less. I am rejoiced that you came whilst I could yet see you. I would like much to see Edward again, but I know that cannot be. It does comfort my heart to know that he is at your court for his fosterage. I fear in my soul that he will never be safe within the reach of his father's paramour."

"Margrethe, it is in our power to wage war against Ethelred, and with just cause. We can easily take from him his little kingdom, and we will, if you so consent. It would be just, for the damage he has done to our daughter."

"If you take his kingdom, what of Edward?"

"Edward would be what he is, our well-loved grandson. He would not be heir to the throne. He would be nephew to your brother William, who would be king over all this land when we are gone."

"Leave Edward his kingdom. Surely my wicked husband is well served being married to Helene. She will bring him only disaster."

"But you, daughter, what of you?"

"I am well here. There is peace in this cottage. Rose and Tammas are good servitors. Karyl is most generous with us."

"You live as a villein."

"No, Father. I live better here than in Torr Castle. Here there is harmony, no court factions stirring trouble, no envious vying for position. This cottage is warmer in the bitter weather than the stone halls of the castle. Rose cooks well, being trained in the kitchens of Karyl's manor. I am pleased to have work to do to fill my days. If I could wish for one thing it would be for music."

"Shall I send Padraik to live with you?"

"That would not be wise. Mayhap from time to time he could come to visit. Then he could bring word of Edward."

"We left Torr Castle this day under the pretext of inspecting the fortifications which Karyl has been making to his manor. We must leave soon, it will be dusk now before we get back to Torr. Should you have a change of heart send word through Karyl to our courts at Winchester. We distrust the wisdom of letting Ethelred continue as king." Alfred kissed his daughter. "Fare you well."

"God go with you, dear Father."

King Alfred called Karyl from the kitchen.

"My thanks, Karyl, for this visit from my father," said Margrethe.

The two men left quickly. Margrethe, she who had been queen and was near blind, was left in the care of the lame and the disfigured.

CHAPTER 9

The visit from her father gave Margrethe a greater measure of peace. She spent more time at her prayers, thanking God for the increase of comfort in their lives.

Rose protested this. "Lady, if things be better for us now, it is because we labor to make them so. Which part of our daily work does God do?"

Tammas was set to carving pattens. He had never seen any, and it was with difficulty that Margrethe communicated the idea of wooden clogs that would keep their feet from the rain puddles and the mud. At her insistence he carved a pair for all three of them. These pattens were removed at the door and saved much mud from being tracked into the cottage.

Rose had seen pattens before but had never thought to own any. She had to admit that it was good to have them. Now her only pair of leather shoes did not get soaked by every rainstorm. She asked, "Lady, why be it that these pattens are not used by all the folk? They cost nothing to make, and last for years."

Margrethe replied, "It must be because the folk do not know how to carve them. Not every man has Tammas' skill with carving. Certes there is no law that says that villeins must go the winter with feet constantly chilled by rain and snow and caked with mud."

It was a new thought for Rose, that the only thing to keep the villeins from a life of greater comfort was a lack of knowing. They had no teaching as to how their lives could be made better or easier. Their masters were never as cruel to them as was the thick layer of ignorance that held them in misery.

The cloth on the loom had grown slowly but steadily. It was a joyful day when the web could be cut free, and the uses for the cloth planned. Tammas got a cloak from it, of which he had much need. He was proud of the garment, and preened himself before the women when they had completed it until they laughed. A king could not have been happier in a new robe. The women debated what to have for themselves. There was enough of the coarse woolen material for either a cloak apiece for them, with some left over, or they could each have a simple new gown. They settled on the gowns. As they cut and stitched the material, which was woven from the wool of their spinning, Rose said, "Lady, I never thought to have so much or live so well. It was a blessed day for me when Karyl brought me to you."

"And who was it who had to teach me to grind the meals, prepare the meat, set the eggs, tend the garden? I learned much from you, Rose."

Edward enjoyed his days of freedom with his father. All too soon his holiday was over. King Alfred was eager to got back to Winchester. Ethelred was reluctant to part with his son so soon, but Helene was nothing loath to see him go.

"The lad is a credit to our house," said Ethelred proudly as he watched his son ride away with the court of King Alfred.

"He does improve, but has far yet to go," replied Helene waspishly. "I shall see that Athelstain is set upon the right path from the very first. Athelstain must have tutors as soon as he can talk. Athelstain must be taught to ride soon after he learns to walk. Athelstain . . ."

King Ethelred walked away. At present Athelstain had not yet shown a desire to either walk or talk. Edward had been attempting both at the age of one year. But Edward came of a different dam. Ethelred was beginning to suspect that Athelstain was a trifle slow due to the bloodline of his mother.

The servitors at Torr Castle were glad to be rid of the company from Winchester. Now they could relax into their slovenly ways. They washed not the drinking cups unless a rim of dirt showed on them. Bread crusts and small bones were swept from the table to be trodden into the rushes on the floor. Safe from disturbance, the spiders draped their pale gray webs in the corners of the dark gray stone walls.

Ethelred, preoccupied with drinking and hunting, gave small heed to the household.

February was ending mild, bringing rain as often as snow by the time that the court of King Alfred had settled back into the castle at Winchester. Edward grumbled at having to resume his studies and his training in manhood. As usual Padraik was the one to whom he carried his problems.

"Padraik, when we were at my castle, at Torr, my sire said that I was heir to the throne and need not groom my pony. Now my grandsire says that *because* I am heir to a throne I must learn to care for my pony."

"Can you not think why?"

"No."

"When you help care for your mount, that animal gets to know you and it will trust you if you are good to it. At present you have but a pony. When you become a man you will have a large stallion, a charger, a destrier to carry you into battle. When you and a horse are together in combat each of you must depend on the other. He must have confidence in your guidance, else he will not obey in time of distress. You must know your mount well enough to know what he likes and dislikes, and how he will react to all situations. Love and confidence cannot be beaten into an animal. You must earn it."

"Oh Padraik, you always think whatever my elders say is right, and whatever I say is wrong."

"Come, now Edward, haven't I given you a fine lute and taught you to play it?"

"Yes. But you don't like the songs I like."

"Such as that 'Fly Song'?"

"Yes."

"That is not good music. Good music makes you feel things in your heart. It lifts you up when you feel sad, and makes you to sing when you are joyous."

"That song made my father joyous!"

"But you are not now with your father. No more of this. If you would be known as a good lute player and a singer, there are many classic ballads you must know. As well there are new ballads being made every day in every land. The beat of these will live and grow into the musical lore of each country. The very best will spread from one country to another. That is why I, as a minnesinger, am pleased to work for your grandfather as a courier. Wherever he sends me on his business I listen to the music of the people, and when I come upon an unusual song I make it my business to learn it. That way I can bring back fresh music to the court. For anyone blessed with the gift of music the learning never ends. My music makes me welcome wherever I go. Now let you begin to learn a new ballad." Padraik's fingers moved on his lute in a simple pattern, which Edward quickly learned to emulate.

March brought scampering clouds and sharp winds that did seem to make a restlessness in the land.

Helene still wondered what had happened with her brother Tom and with Olfin, who had both disappeared from Torr Castle when Margrethe did. That they were employed in a plot to do away with Margrethe, Helene knew. Had they managed to dispose of the queen and then gone into exile so that none would suspect them? Had they abducted the queen and gone to live abroad with her as a mistress or a hostage? It was not likely that Margrethe could have escaped from the clutches of Olfin and Tom when her two gallants had been so battered in the battle. Nonetheless, Helene was perturbed. If the former queen lives, then Helene was no queen, nor even a wife. Her child had but a pale hope at best of attaining the throne. If Margrethe were not dead, then Athelstain's claim to the throne would become very weak. Athelstain was but one of many sons Ethelred had begotten outside the marriage bed. Edward was still the primary heir to the throne. But Edward, in Winchester, was beyond Helene's reach.

Helene resolved to eliminate the bastards of Ethelred's that she could readily identify. She now had a steward, Radnar, whom she trusted completely. The only right or wrong Radnar could distinguish was if a deed put gold into his purse or no. Helene called Radnar to her. "Wist you that our king has not always sown his seed wisely?"

"His majesty has sown as the lust took him."

"A full crop of weeds have grown up which could possibly cut off the sunlight from the grain."

"Your highness would like the field weeded?"

"I would. Wild growth never makes for good harvest."

"The task will not be difficult. Children do fall into streams. They run beneath the hooves of frightened horses. They wander away into the woods. They nibble poison berries or mushrooms. None need ever know that our hand has been set to the task of weeding. How much will you pay?"

When a price had been agreed on, Radnar asked, "Once the field is weeded, what then? Will not more wild seed be sown?" This was a thought for Helene to ponder.

Before Radnar could begin his weeding, fate began its weeding of all the children in the land. An epidemic of what were called maseles spread high and low, sparing neither castle nor hovel from its spots.

Edward awakened one morning, saying that he did not feel well. Yet he ate his bread and drank his ale for breakfast, and asked for more.

King Alfred said, "Word was brought to us that you did not feel well. Your appetite does not bear that out. How feel you now?"

"Still hungry. Please, can I have more?"

King Alfred watched as Edward gobbled every crumb and drank the last drop of his ale. "How now?"

"I just stay hungry. Please, grandsires can I have more bread and ale? And perhaps a sausage?"

"If you will eat it all, and waste nothing."

Edward quickly ate all of his third serving of breakfast.

"Had enough now?"

"Not really. I must be growing bigger to need so much to eat."

"We say you have had enough. Go find your tutor, and get on with your Latin studies."

As the morn progressed Edward found concentration very difficult. Before midday his eyes ached, and his legs felt tired. When he went for his lesson with Padraik his face was flushed bright scarlet. Padraik put a hand on Edward's forehead and found him to be burning with fever.

"Come boy," said Padraik, leading him from the room.

"Come where?"

"Let's get you to the infirmary. You are ill."

Before they reached the infirmary Edward was aware of a roaring noise in his head. He was glad to lie down quickly and let someone else remove his shoes and leggings. He was so hot and thirsty.

As the fever rose, delirium began. Villeins were stacking endless shocks of grain. Higher, higher, higher. Huge boars with curving tusks and glowing red eyes tore down the stacks. Edward tried to cry a protest. Padraik spoke soothingly to him. Edward could see the villeins rebuilding the stacks of grain and Padraik at the same time.

"Ice. Please, Padraik, is there ice?"

Padraik sponged the small burning body with cool water.

"Ice. Please, Padraik, ice."

"There is no ice."

"Water. Cold water."

Padraik carefully held up the boy's head, and gave him a drink of cool water.

King Alfred's infirmarian protested, "Cool water could kill the child. With such fever he should have hot drinks. Cold water could give him a stomach chill."

Edward seemed slightly relieved after the cool water. He fell asleep. Padraik sponged him off again and was pleased to see the red spots were coming out well. The maseles covered the chest and back and were beginning to appear on Edward's face.

Edward was lucid the next morn when King Alfred came to see him.

"Well, lad, the next time you have such an appetite we will send you straight here to the infirmary."

"How look my maseles?"

"You are as spotted as a robin's egg."

"Wish I could see me."

"It will only be a few days now until you will be up again. God be with you."

"And with you, Grandsire."

King Alfred gave thought to the concern that his daughter must be having regarding the health of her son. The maseles had killed many children, deafened some, blinded others. He decided to send Padraik to Margrethe to give her news of Edward's safe recovery.

At Torr Castle Athelstain had not been as fortunate as Edward. His case of maseles had produced a mastoid infection. His ears hurt him dreadfully before they began to drain copious amounts of yellow pus. When he began to recover, it was evident that he could hear very little. This seemed to stir a hatred in Helene, so that at the time when Athelstain was most in need of a mother's comfort she gave him only harsh words, interspersed with impatient slaps. Athelstain withdrew into himself a little more each day. He was a lonely, silent child in a lonely, silent world.

Only his joy in eating remained. Athelstain ate and drank all he could get and grew heavy and lethargic.

Helene would gladly have born another child. However Ethelred avoided her bed, as a rule. It was now a rare occasion when the combination of lust, drink, and Helene's availability lured Ethelred to her chamber.

☦ ☦ ☦

King Alfred had another reason for dispatching Padraik as courier at this time. A strange ship had berthed at Porchester, which was said to carry goods from the Orient. King Alfred wanted a true report on the ship and its cargo.

Padraik found the vessel without difficulty. It was black with two large eyes painted on the prow. It was easily the largest ship in the harbor. A guard of soldiers was preventing the crew from leaving the ship. They also prevented any Englishman from boarding the ship.

Padraik left Small John on the dock and showed his commission from King Alfred to the guards. They let him board the ship, where he was surrounded by suspicious, swarthy men.

Padraik tried speaking to them in Latin. No response. German fared no better. French the same. Because he had learnt but little of it, Padraik waited until last to try the tongue of Espagnia.

To Padraik's halting Spanish the swarthy men responded in a perfect flood of language. They were Moors from southern Spain, their ship a merchant vessel searching for new markets. They carried a cargo of golden fruits, which Padraik had seen before on a visit to Italy. The golden apples of legend, these were said to be with tough skins, juicy interiors, and small hard pips in each segment. The Moors had also brought silks from the Orient and cloves from the island of Madagascar. They said that their intended port had been Londinium.

Padraik deduced from their use of the old Roman name for London that they must be using old Roman maps for guidance. Small wonder then that they had arrived at the wrong harbor. The Roman maps Padraik had seen required a pilot who knew the territory if they were to be followed in safety. Padraik sent one of the guardsmen to Winchester with a true report of this ship. Then he arranged stabling with the garrison mounts for Small John. Taking his lute with him, Padraik rejoined the crew aboard the vessel.

When he opened his lute case, the Moors exclaimed over the lovely instrument. Two of their group went running to fetch pipes and a tabor. The others seated themselves on the deck. First Padraik gave them a lively contra dance tune which set them to clapping in time to it. Then he tried a ballad, a tale of thwarted love, heroic fighting, much sighing, and some dying. It was in a slightly minor key, which the Moors seemed to like.

Motioning for Padraik to be still, the piper and the tabor player began a complicated, wailing tune with a variable rhythm. The key was strange to Padraik, full of quick trills and quarter-tones that slid into dissonance on the untrained ear. This piece was followed by another very like it, in which the crew joined in singing. Padraik was sitting, just listening, when he was inspected by a small animal. The animal, scarce two hands tall, was covered with long gray fur. It had a short muzzle, large erect rounded ears, long whiskers, and a medium long tail. It walked around Padraik silently, sniffing and sniffing. Seeming to approve, it climbed into his lap and curled up. He put a hand on it, and found a vibration coming from its throat. The Moors sitting near seemed to approve of the little beast's actions. They attempted to explain the animal to Padraik. "Gato," they said. This he knew to mean catte. "Muertan los ratones." The Moors pantomimed fiercely the little beast catching and killing rodents. Padraik was acquainted with the wild cattes of his own land, but they were nothing like this sweetly singing animal.

The master of the ship invited Padraik to share his quarters for the night, which he did gladly. Padraik marveled at the luxury with which the cabin was appointed. Rich carpets on the floor drinking vessels of silver, lanthorns with shades of pierced metal that made geometric patterns of light on the walls. He would gladly have spent more than one night here. Unhappily for him, a cavalcade from Winchester arrived the next day. And with it, the king.

King Alfred examined the cargo and ordered the purchase of the entire lot.

The Moors had hoped to pick up a return cargo, but the English had nothing at Porchester to trade. The Moors purchased some sheep and fowl to provide fresh meat on their homeward journey. Padraik discovered that the catte had six kits and desired to purchase two of them. These the master placed in a small woven basket and presented them to Padraik as a gift.

The ship sailed on the tide. The master was well pleased with the price for his cargo.

Padraik resumed his journey to Margrethe, carrying the basket with the two kits and a bag of golden apples.

CHAPTER 10

Tammas and Rose had not met Padraik before he made this journey to the cottage with the kits and the golden apples. Margrethe was delighted to welcome her old friend and confidant for a visit. She had been much concerned over Edward and was pleased to hear of his safe recovery from the maseles. Tammas had grown accustomed to getting all of the attention from the two women and regarded Padraik as an unwanted rival for their affections. Rose grumbled about the extra work having a visitor made, but she enjoyed Padraik's music entirely. When he began playing simple folk melodies Rose began to sing with him. She proved to have a warm, sweet voice.

"Rose, you've been with me for over a year now, and have never sung before," said Margrethe.

"Lady, you must recall that much of that time we had little to sing about," replied Rose.

Tammas looked at the two gray kits and pronounced them "boy-brudder and girl-sister." Gray Boy and Gray Girl they became. The kits adjusted quickly to their new home, and romped wildly up and down the stairs, across beds, under stools, climbing the legs of the table, the loom, and the gowns of the women in their happy games. Margrethe was loath to discipline them. Rose grumbled even more about the disturbance that they caused. In truth, the kits did but little harm and provided hours of entertainment. A sudden silence would fall upon the cottage, and the kits would be found curled together in exhausted sleep. Vitality quickly restored, they awakened to race and play heartily again. They caused Margrethe to laugh more than she had done in the past year.

"How long is your visit to us to be?" asked Margrethe of Padraik.

"Your father said that I may remain a fortnight. Then I am to return by way of the seashore and check on the additions which he ordered to be made to the shore fortifications. Your father does expect a full invasion of the Norsemen."

Rose turned green and felt ill at the very word "Norseman." Tammas looked none too happy himself.

Margrethe said, "Until the Norsemen really do come, let us not fear shadows. After all, the woods are full of adders, yet we walked there without worry. The world holds many evil men, but that does not destroy our love and trust in our friends. If our deeds be good, and our hands be innocent, surely our God will preserve us."

The next week the weather turned unexpectedly warm. King Ethelred was delighted. Perfect weather for fresh hunting adventures! From the northern portion of his kingdom he had received reports of large herds of deer and of several wolfpacks, which had found the tame sheep of the villeins to be easy targets for their stalking skills.

Ethelred resolved to go on a long hunt, spending several nights in tents, and having sport in chasing the wolves. He commanded that his nobles, including Karyl, should accompany him on the hunt.

Helene called Radnar to her privately. "My spouse does go to sport against the wolves. Where wolves do gather there may be danger to kings. Is this not true?"

"Very true, your royal Highness."

"Fang and claw are lethal, but less so than iron-shod arrows and spears."

"True."

"Many an accident happens in a hunt, with arrows which miss the game and strike other hunters."

"Such does happen."

"Even a king, without his armor, could fall prey to such an accident."

"That is possible."

"Then see you to it."

"What is the reward?"

"Have I been less than generous?"

"Never. But never has the game been so large."

"When my son is crowned king, you shall be appointed a noble fief."

"And money now?"

"And money now! None in the kingdom shall have more of wealth and lands than you, Radnar."

Radnar, counting his wealth in this thoughts, went forth to prepare for his largest hunt.

On his way to join the hunting party at Torr Castle, Karyl stopped by the cottage to visit Margrethe. He had brought the needles and embroidery threads she had requested. When Karyl arrived at the cottage Padraik was playing his lute, Tammas whittling away at a bit of wood, Rose spinning, Margrethe weaving, and the gray kits romping through the rooms. It was a scene of peaceful domestic activity that made Karyl suddenly aware of how much his life had been lacking since the death of his wife.

"Will you stay to dine with us?" asked Margrethe.

"Nay. That would please me much, but I am bidden to attend the king on a hunt."

"Rose baked special honeycakes this morn. I knew that you would come this day. As my eyesight has been fading, I see more and more often pictures of the things which will happen during the day. Not with my eyes, I see it inside my head. Like an awake dreaming. I like not this affair of the hunt. I have seen much danger in it, and not to the animals."

Karyl made light of her fears. "Every day has danger in it for every man. We are born to it, and die in it. Now, for the nonce, could I have some of those honeycakes, and a bit of music from Padraik before I ride? We are commanded to assemble at the castle at midday."

When Karyl rode away Margrethe sighed. Her foreboding of danger increased. Someone would die, and not from the beasts. God grant that the victim be not Karyl!

☩ ☩ ☩

It was a large force of men who gathered for the wolf hunt. Each noble brought with him a least two servants to care for his horses, his weapons, and his tent and to cook his food. Ethelred provided several wagons drawn by sturdy draft horses to carry the tents and heavy gear. As the group set forth from Torr Castle they resembled an army more than a hunting party.

Athelstain was standing at an upstairs window, excited by all the horses and men. He waved frantically at them as they rode away, but none saw him to return his waving. When Athelstain began to weep in childish disappointment, a nursemaid stuffed an oatcake in his mouth. Distracted, he soon forgot the cause of his tears.

The hunt rode due north, crossing the River Stour by the bridge at Blanford, thence to Tarrant Hinton for the night. They made a circular encampment, with watch fires set along the perimeter. The horses grazed under the none-too-cautious care of the sleepy servants, while the noble knights enjoyed the fellowship that such open living induces.

Dawn found them stirring, early birdsong having given the alarm that day was near. Even so, it was mid-morn before they had breakfasted, packed tents and supplies, mounted up, and headed farther into the rolling hill country. Gorse brambles, and thorn abounded here. Good cover for wild beasts. Except for an occasional hare, they disturbed little game as they rode. This fact Ethelred blamed on the depredations of the wolves. When the hunt reached a well-forested area, Ethelred said, "This will be the location of our central camp. From here we will ride out each day in a different direction until we locate the packs of wolves."

Once the central camp had been set up, the servants of the nobles began to raid the farms and villas nearby, taking the stores of grain by right of the Royal Hunt. Chickens and pigs were collected also. Their rightful owners had no recourse except to pray that the hunt would soon depart.

Unwilling to draw attention to himself, Radnar stayed well back from the hunt. He could follow their trail with ease a day after they had passed. It seemed the better course not to show himself. He rode alone, without fear. Whom could he possibly meet more evil than himself?

A league away from the central campsite Radnar found an angry villein who was quite willing to relay false information to the Royal Hunt in exchange for a small coin.

Karyl rode to give this villein's report to the king. "Majesty, a villein came with the news of a wolfpack which dens up in a small vale between those two low hills on the right."

"Stay with us, Karyl," said King Ethelred. To his royal trumpeter he called, "Blow for a gathering charge to the right." The trumpeter blew, and even as his horn sounded Ethelred said, "Now ride beside us Karyl, and good sport be ours."

Karyl rode at the right hand of the king, letting the king lead by two paces. The track to the two hills was good, and they galloped full speed into the declivity. Suddenly an iron-tipped arrow took Ethelred through the chest, piercing the left lung and his heart. Ethelred fell as a second arrow grazed the mane of Karyl's mount. Karyl flattened himself against the horse as a third arrow intended for his own heart swished past. Karyl stopped his horse and stood in the stirrups to give the ancient rallying cry of Torr Castle, "A king. A king!" Hearing his call, the other nobles rode quickly to them.

A confusion of questions shouted. "Who did this deed?" "What happened?" "Is the king dead?" "Whose arrow is through the king?"

From the style of the fletching the arrow must have come from the armory at Torr Castle. So had the arrows of most of the other nobles. Very few, like Karyl, had their own fletcher. There was no way of telling whose quiver had held this deadly bolt.

The destrier of the king was standing near its fallen owner, as it had been trained to do. Several of the nobles lifted up their dead king and draped him across the saddle. Slowly and solemnly, they walked their steeds back to the central camp.

When he reached his own tent, Karyl hastily wrote a message to King Alfred.

> *Ethelred slain. Guard Edward well. On no account is he to come to Torr without armed troops. There is treachery here.*

Karyl dispatched one of his personal servants with the messages, lending the man his own powerful horse, the better to reach Winchester more than ten leagues away. The servant would have to stop for the night to rest the horse. There was no way before morning that the word could reach Winchester. If a cavalcade set out from Winchester immediately on receiving the news, it would take them a minimum of two days to reach Torr. Perhaps three days, depending on the weather.

Karyl sat on his cot and thought. That this evil deed had been hatched by Helene, he did not doubt. Her ambition to put her son on the throne, infant though he was, was her all-consuming passion. Karyl would try to delay the return to Torr as long as possible. In all decency, the new king could not be hailed before the old king was buried.

The nobles were milling around their dead king in want of a leader. Karyl suggested, "Could the king not be laid out in dignity upon one of the wagons? Fitted out in the best clothing he has brought with him? Let him be washed and combed, and alum-water rubbed into his face to help preserve it. Then we could make a royal procession.

We could move slowly through all of the nearby villages, letting the people see their slain monarch. As we go, we can ask word concerning any stranger in the area who may have done this deed."

Relieved to have someone make a decision for them, the other nobles willingly fell in with Karyl's plan. They began wrangling over which towns to divert the royal procession through. Karyl left them to it. The more time they spent deciding on the route, the better.

Each of the nobles felt it would be an honor to have the dead king's procession pass through a town on his particular fief. This would never be feasible. There were too many of them, and the body of the king would putrefy long before all were visited. After many hours, a zigzag course was agreed on. The route would go north to Shaftesberig, which was only four leagues away. Thence southwest to Sturminster Newton, southeast to Blanford, southwest to Whitchurch, southeast to Bore Regis, and south to Torr. Moving at a funeral pace, each town would take a day to reach. They would be back at Torr Castle by evening of the sixth day.

Karyl was well pleased by this. King Alfred would have ample time to reach Torr Castle before them. He asked, "Who has sent word to Helene that she is now widowed?" None had. Knowing too well Helene's volatile nature, not one of the nobles would volunteer to bring her the news. If the news were brought by a servant, Helene could well order such a bearer of bad tidings to the dungeons or to death. None among the nobles desired to sacrifice a servant to Helene's whims. Yet she must be told. They settled the issue by drawing lots. A hapless servant was dispatched to Torr.

Karyl wondered privately how many of the nobles felt as he did that Helene needed no telling. This deed must have been of her planning.

At the abbey in Shaftesberig a coffin was purchased for Ethelred's body. The coffin was left open, displaying the dead king, until they reached Sturminster Newton. After this, the lid was fastened down. The odors of the corpse had grown strong, too strong to invite close viewing of the body.

The nobles seemed to rather enjoy being the center of attention for all of the populace of the region as the procession zigzagged on its way.

When they reached Bere Regis, Karyl left the group. He was within two leagues of his home manor. Other nobles had dropped out along the route. None envied those whose task it was to deliver the corpse to Helene.

Karyl went first to the cottage at Swinstig. The occupants had already heard a rumor that something had gone amiss at the hunt, Karyl gave them a first hand account of the death of Ethelred. Margrethe burst into tears. Karyl regarded her with some surprise.

"My lady, after what that man attempted to do to you, you would weep for him?"

"It matters not what he has done. He was the husband of my body, and the father of my child. Ethelred was not really evil, just of a nature too weak to resist any temptation. When we were first wed he cherished me. It is for this that I mourn him."

Rose went to place a protective arm around Margrethe. "Lady, please don't weep more. Your eyes are too dim now to blind them further with tears."

"How can I not weep, knowing that Ethelred went to his death unshriven? Am I then to rejoice at the eternal torment of his soul?"

Margrethe made an effort to stem her tears, then said, "Look at the sins for which he must atone. Murder and attempted murder, adultery with many outside his marriage bed. A bigamous marriage. Covetousness, gluttony, and drunkenness. When I was being schooled at the abbey of the Benedictines, these last three alone were considered to be cause enough for damnation."

Mopping a few last tears, Margrethe regained her composure.

"Rose, we have not offered our visitor any refreshment. Let Tammas assist you in preparing a repast. Padraik, get out your lute and make us sad music. Let us think gently of him who is dead."

CHAPTER 11

Early on the morn Padraik made ready to depart.

"Were you not given leave to remain for a fortnight?" asked Margrethe.

"Yes. But think you, would it not be wise if I were to arrive at Torr Castle with the court from Winchester when they do come for the funeral?"

Margrethe smiled, "You were ever clever, Padraik! Were I yet queen I would give you a royal commission to carry a message to my father. As it falls, I can but ask you for a kindness."

"Speak on, my lady."

"Then listen well. Tell my father that I will fashion the linen shurte for Edward to wear under his robe at his coronation. As Edward's mother, this will be my joy."

"Have you time to weave the linen?"

"Had you not noticed? My loom was set with linen long before you came to visit. When the hens in our fowl yard began laying well, Rose deprived our household of eggs for ten days. She carried the eggs to her old village to barter for flax ready for the spinning. Now I need but weave for a short time longer to have enough linen for the shurte for Edward."

"Be mindful that Edward has grown much since last you saw him."

"How large is my son now?"

Measuring a height against the doorframe, Padraik said, "He stands this tall. And has grown quite sturdy."

Tears stood in Margrethe's eyes as she said, "Would that I could see my son again, just once." Her lips trembled, but she controlled them into a faint smile. "Such be the lot our Lord has given us. Let us break our fast before you depart. Karyl will carry the shurte to Torr Castle in full time for the coronation."

☩ ☩ ☩

At Torr Castle the body of Ethelred had been transferred from the wooden coffin to his stone sarcophagus.

Soon after their marriage, Ethelred and Margrethe had ordered their sarcophagus made with their effigies on the lids. Now the slender stone figure of Ethelred, lying on the lid in full battle dress, with sword in one hand, scepter in the other, crown upon his head, bore little resemblance to the bloated dissolute man Ethelred had been at his death.

Margrethe had been carved in her most regal gown, with a flowing wimple and a coronal. Helene had ordered that the lid with Margrethe's carved effigy be broken up. A new lid was now being prepared by the stonemasons—a lid with an effigy of Helene.

At the present time, the sarcophagus of Ethelred was to be in the chapel of Torr Castle until time for the state funeral. Then it would be loaded onto a wagon and taken to the church of St. Christopher on Lychtminster Hill. There would Ethelred rest, through all time to come near to his father and grandfather, whose sarcophagi stood against the interior of the front wall of the chapel. There, the light entering through the narrow windows of stained glass cast a strange mottled red and blue glow over their effigies.

Helene had received the body of her husband with a well-feigned grief. She wailed and berated those who had gone on the wolf hunt with Ethelred. She shrieked and moaned over the corpse for one day, then ceased. There was much for her to attend. If she moved swiftly, mayhap she could have herself recognized as regent, to rule until Edward came of age. It was a worthy goal. Helene had no intention to inform either Edward or King Alfred of the death of Ethelred until it would be too late for them to attend the funeral.

Helene had messages sent throughout the kingdom to inform of the day set for the funeral. She ordered the castle kitchens to prepare a huge amount of food for the funeral celebration, enough to last for several days for all of the noble visitors. Then she retired to her rooms in company with her ladies and spent much time in deciding what to wear for the ceremonies which were to come. A gown of black silk was being sewn for her, embroidered richly with gold threads. Black lace as fine as cobwebs formed her mourning veil. And only one now stood in the path of Athelstain becoming king—only Edward.

The court at Winchester had the news of Ethelred's death within two days. The courier sent by Karyl had ridden swiftly and changed horses often on the way.

When the courier had delivered his message to King Alfred the king called for his grandson to be brought to the audience chamber of the castle.

"Edward, lad, you are now a king. Do you understand what I say to you?"

"Yes, grandsire," replied the child as his face went pale. "You mean that my father is dead," Edward trembled, and Alfred put an arm around him.

"There, Edward, weep if you so desire. It is not unmanly to weep when a father dies."

"Mayhap not, but he would not have liked that. Did he fall in battle with a foe?"

"No. He was most treacherously slain from ambush. None saw the craven who pulled the bow which brought him down."

"He was at Torr?"

"Nay. He was leading the hunt for a pack of wolves which had been terrorizing the northern part of his lands."

"Grandsire, when I was smaller and desired to learn to play the lute, I thought it to be easy until I tried it. Now I have not the desire to be king. I think it be too difficult."

"King you are by right of heritage. Have no fears of the difficulties. No one would expect you to be regent now. Others will rule in your name until you are older."

"Much older?"

"Until you are sixteen."

Edward stopped trembling. Alfred summoned the tutor to take the boy to his room. As he walked numbly obedient with the tutor, Edward's thoughts cried out, *Oh Padraik, Padraik, I need you with me now!*

Padraik was hurrying toward Winchester as fast as Small John could travel. Padraik had reasoned that if he kept to the main highway he would be bound to meet with the cavalcade from Winchester.

Padraik was yet ten leagues from Winchester when he saw the cavalcade moving toward him. More than 200 warriors mounted on swift horses surrounding the new boy king and his grandfather as they rode with full pomp. The battle flag of Alfred, as well as the flags of Wessex and Sussex were displayed on a dozen staffs carried by outriders. All of the horses were caparisoned as if for battle. The men rode in full armor, their burnished shields glittering in the sunlight. They were followed by equerries, grooms, the band of relief horses, and baggage carts.

Edward gave a shout of joy when he espied Padraik. He left his grandfather and rode to fling himself heedlessly into Padraik's arms. Small John staggered from this unexpected extra burden.

"Oh Padraik," cried Edward. "Now I must learn to be king! And I hadn't finished yet learning to be a prince."

"There, child, you will master it easily. You have but to look at your grandsire for your example."

"Will you help me?"

"I? What know I about being king?"

"You always know everything."

"Nay lad. It is because you are so young that you speak so. I will help you as much as your grandsire will wish, but I am his man. You will have many men of your own to aid you."

"And women to help, too?"

"Yes, if you wish. Why do you ask?"

"My grandsire has three women riding in the baggage carts now."

"Does he?"

"Yes. They are skilled with the needle, and are cutting and sewing my coronation robe when we stop to rest on this journey."

"Return to your own mount now, Edward. I would have speech with your grandfather."

Signaling for the group to continue on their way, King Alfred rode out of the protective horde of warriors. He and Padraik fell in at the rear of the entourage. First making certain that no one else was within earshot, King Alfred requested, "Tell us truly, how did Ethelred die?"

"I know not much, I was with Margrethe when Karyl arrived with the news of his death. From what Karyl related, he was the only one near the king when Ethelred was shot. Karyl's horse was slightly wounded when an arrow grazed its neck. You must wait until Karyl can give you his account to know fully what did happen. Your royal daughter sends you greetings, and bids me to say that she is making the shurte for Edward to wear under his coronation robes."

"Is that wise?"

"It is her heart's desire. Karyl will bring the shurte when he meets us at Torr."

Small John stumbled in his weariness.

"May I beg a favor, Majesty?"

"Certes."

"Is there another mount I can use? Small John has been pushed too hard to continue riding him. He will be jaded soon."

Alfred motioned to a servitor, "See that Padraik has the pick of the extra mounts for his use."

Padraik went with the servitor as the king returned to his place in the center of the column. The colorful procession continued its course on the old Roman road from Winchester.

At Torr Castle the main hall was in an uproar. "Dastard, dolt, and fool!" shouted Helene at a courier, "How is it you dare to bear such a message to me? The bishop cannot come, indeed!" She aimed a blow at the courier who dodged it easily.

Father John demurred, "Your majesty, it were well not to cause harm to the bishop's man." Father John spoke calmly to the courier. "Had the bishop other words for us?"

"He had. The bishop will bend every effort to arrive as soon as it is mortally possible for him to do. His intent is to be here for the coronation of the new king."

"Where is His Reverence?"

"The bishop is in York, whither he was called to preside over an ecclesiastical convocation. Past riders took him the news of King Ethelred's death. His great age, now well past seventy years, makes haste impossible for him. He has set out, and will arrive in a seven day or more."

"And that is too late," cried Helene loudly. "Much too late. I set the funeral ceremony for two days hence." Her brow clouded with anger.

"My lady queen," said Father John. "The prayers of the church will be the same for the dead, no matter if the bishop or myself do lead them."

Helene covered her face, and feigned to weep. "All do conspire to prevent a proper honor being shown to him who was my very heart." She sobbed and bleated noisily until Father John took the courier from the room. Then Helene betook herself to the kitchens to create a minor hell among the workers there.

✢ ✢ ✢

Rose watched in amazement as Margrethe wove a complicated design into the end of the linen they had made. It was composed of an R intertwined with a crown, repeated many times across the width of the material.

"Lady, there be not many could weave as fine as that," Rose exclaimed.

"You could learn it, Rose. I was schooled in it by the good sisters at the abbey. They often do much more complicated designs to dress the altars."

"I have never seen such fine work, lady. It be a pity that your sight is going. When you can no longer see, none here will know how to weave like this."

Margrethe worked steadily a few more hours, then called, "Come aid me, Rose, in cutting this free from the loom. Now we have the proper material to make the coronation shurte for my son."

Margrethe cut the linen into the shapes needed. However, Rose had to do most of the stitching. Margrethe could no longer see to do fine stitching, no matter how close she held it to her eyes. Working together, the two women had the shurte completed in good time for Karyl to collect it on his way to Torr.

When the first outriders of King Alfred's cavalcade arrived at Torr Castle, the gatekeeper was reluctant to admit them to the castle yard. When the main body of warriors arrived the gatekeeper argued no longer. The gates were opened wide, and the horde rode through.

Taken by surprise, Helene stood silent as she watched the travelers from Winchester trooping into the castle. King Alfred here, and Edward, as well would mean that she must speak and act with caution. She dispatched servants to prepare rooms for the unexpected guests. Then she set her lips in a determined smile, and went out to take Edward by the hand. She looked the solemn lad in the eye as she said, "Welcome home, my son. We have suffered a sad loss. You a father, me a beloved husband. But you stand not alone, for I will ever be mother to you."

Edward regarded her stonily. "Madame, it is true that we have both suffered a loss by the death of my father. My mother is also dead. I do not want another."

King Alfred said, "Our journey has been tiring, for we came in all haste that Edward not miss the funeral of his father. Can we be shown to our chambers? We will have much to discuss with you after we dine this night."

Helene summoned servants to lead them to their appointed rooms. Then she sat fuming. Who had informed Edward that his father was dead? And King Alfred, with his large retinue including those three "sewing women," if that, indeed, was what they were, obviously intending to see that the boy was crowned king of Wessex. That the boy was yet so young could mayhap be turned to a benefit. Perhaps Helene could be one of the council that would rule for the boy until he came of age. If any did object to a woman as one of the council, then mayhap she could have Radnar elected to it. But could she still trust him fully? Of late he had developed a greedy, crafty look. He was a man to use, to watch, but not to trust. And when she had no further need of him, what then?

Edward and his grandfather were shown to the large suite of rooms that had been used by Ethelred. Edward was so weary that he lay down on the bed and was asleep instantly.

He awakened from his nap to see little Athelstain moving about the room, curiously examining everything. Edward said, "What do you, child?" No response from Athelstain. Edward spoke louder, "I questioned you. What do you here?" Athelstain continued his investigation. Angered now, Edward roared, "Even if you are my brother, you get out of my things!" These loud angry words penetrated Athelstain's deafness. He heard them faintly, and turned to smile at Edward. Athelstain was the image of his father. The square jaw, pale blue eyes, and the shape of his skull were undeniable proof of his paternity.

Athelstain's nurse rushed into the room. "Your pardon for the child's intrusion. I did but turn my back and he was gone."

"He does not hear well?"

"No. Ever since he had the maseles he has heard very little. I will take him away now." She scooped Athelstain up in her arms.

Edward leaned close to the child, and screamed, "Brother Athelstain, go in peace!"

Athelstain gave a wide grin and said, "Bubba. Bubba."

The nurse beamed with delight, "He hasn't spoken since the maseles." She went away still talking, but Athelstain drowned out her voice in his roars of temper over being taken to his own room.

Until this day Edward had only felt a jealous contempt for his brother. That emotion was now banished by pity. Poor wight! His father dead, Helene his mother, and unable to hear anything quieter than thunder. Edward felt so very fortunate. His mother had been a lovely, gentle queen, for all the mockery given her after the unfortunate accident to her eyes with the poisoned yarn. His grandsire was strong and wise. And there was Padraik. Thinking of Padraik turned Edward's thoughts again to Athelstain. The child would never be able to enjoy music; never hear the sounds of harp, lute, or pipes; never know the songs of birds.

Edward was tidying himself when King Alfred returned. The king ordered a basin of hot water brought and washed the grime of the journey from his face and hands. As he was combing his beard and hair he said, "It would be well if you also washed yourself, Edward."

"Am I not neat?"

"Neat, yes. Clean, no. Dirt is no ornament to the face and hands."

Edward found the warm water soothing to his skin. As he was patting himself dry he said, "Grandsire, did you know my little brother cannot hear?"

"Athelstain? No. He is deaf?"

"So says his nurse. He had the maseles when I did, and now hears only great noises. Plain speech he cannot hear at all."

King Alfred looked thoughtful, but all he said was, "Come along, now. The company awaits us before they can dine."

"Are we late?"

"Nay," King Alfred smiled at the boy, "Whenever two kings, such as we and thou, choose to dine, that is the proper time to eat. The company may assemble early but kings are never late."

Together they walked down the steep stone stairs of the King's Tower. Alfred led the boy to the great chair and motioned him to sit. Edward turned a white face and tear-filled eyes to his grandfather. "I cannot. Not in the seat of my father."

"Then we will sit there, and you beside us. Come, let the food be served."

By dawn of the day of Ethelred's funeral the gatekeeper was busy challenging and admitting party after party of nobles and others who came to pay final homage to the dead king. Among them was Karyl, bearing Margrethe's gift for her son.

Noon was the time set for the funeral cortege to set out for St. Christopher's. It took ten strong men to carry the sarcophagus from the castle chapel to the waiting wagon. The team of huge draft horses moved the wagon slowly, bumping unevenly across the tournament yard and out onto the high road. The stone paving of this roadway made a smooth surface for the ironbound wagon wheels to roll on. Helene, Edward, and King Alfred held their horses to a walk as they rode slowly behind the wagon, Edward thought that all the kingdom must have turned out to join in the procession. The mounted mourners were arranged by rank, lowliest in the rear. Those who had no horses walked. For two hours they trudged slowly along.

All in the land could participate in this occasion. Having so little diversion in their lives, serfs and villeins flocked to join the procession. To walk in the funeral procession of a king was to have an important story to recount one day to their grandchildren.

When the procession was halfway up the Lychtminster Hill, Father John began the *Miserere* chant. The courtiers, the nobles, the followers on foot all gradually were drawn into the mournful chant.

> *Have mercy, have mercy, Lord God,*
> *On a soul new-come before you.*
> *Have mercy, have mercy, Lord God*
> *May it be purged from sin.*
> *Have mercy, have mercy, Lord God*
> *Let Paradise be its eternal home.*
> *Have mercy, have mercy, Lord God.*

Inside the church a sturdy bier had been set in the nave, where the sarcophagus would rest during the service of the funeral mass. The pallbearers wrestled their heavy burden onto this bier while Father John changed from his traveling gown to his silken ceremonial robe and stole. A choir of monks from the small abbey at Newcross had come to chant the responses.

The endless chanting, the packed crowd in the church, and the incense fumes all combined to make Edward feel faint. He leaned on his grandfather for support and comfort.

Helene sat proudly in her rich mourning gown, the fine veil masking her sharp glances around the church. Her ladies sat around her.

The congregation inside the church shuffled and shifted position often during the three-hour service. Outside the church, the serfs and villeins sat on the ground, listening to as much of the service as they could hear through the open door. When at last the service ended, all were thankful.

The now-empty wagon moved briskly along on the road home. The pace of the returning procession was much faster than it had been when going toward the church. Even so, darkness fell before they arrived at Torr. Dark night, with no moon to light the way. Torches were lighted along the length of the procession to show the road. Forever after, when he thought of his father's funeral Edward would recall most clearly that line of bright torches as they wound their way through the black of night.

CHAPTER 12

Margrethe and Tammas had not joined in the funeral march for Ethelred. Margrethe because she feared being discovered, Tammas because of his lame leg. Rose had joined with the villeins from Swinstig for the long walk.

It had been a sunny, pleasant day. The cottage doors stood open, and the two gray kits raced in and out exuberantly. They ran through the garden, each in a different furrow, feigning surprise when coming together at the end of a row of peas. They danced stifflegged up to one another in mock anger, tails fluffed, then ran indoors for a brief nap together before resuming their antics.

Rose had cared for the chickens before she set out. Tammas had worked willingly at hoeing the weeds from the garden until he became overheated by the sun. The remainder of the day he spent limping to the front door, peering out, and asking, "When that woman coming home?"

Margrethe prayed all of the prayers for the dead she had learned from the Benedictine nuns. She sat spinning and praying, weaving and praying until late in the afternoon. Then, feeling that the funeral was over, she went to sit on the back doorstep and enjoy the last of the sunlight. The kits came to nestle in her lap.

Tammas limped out to feed the fowls. He came back grumbling, "That woman still not home!"

Margrethe said, "Tammas, you have behaved this day like a jealous husband, whose wife is too long away at a market fair. Are you then so fond of Rose?"

"No! Not like that woman much. Need her. Woman gone, Tammas does everything. Now Tammas cook." He stumped away to build up the hearth fire.

They dined before the long twilight ended. Margrethe said, "No need to worry about Rose. She is with the other people from Swinstig. She is returning now."

"Not worry about that woman. Want her here to work. Tammas not do everything she here."

When at last the sounds of the returning villagers could be heard, Tammas smiled broadly. The sound of Rose's footsteps caused him to turn his chair toward the hearth and begin whittling industriously.

Rose came in, tired but enlivened by her outing.

Margrethe said, "Get yourself some food, then come tell us of the day. We missed you much."

"Not me," said Tammas, "I not miss you, woman."

The inhabitants of Torr Castle were late in rising on the morn. All were wearied by the long funeral of the previous day. Edward awakened and made his way to the chapel, while his grandfather still slept. Father John was in the chapel, alone at his prayers. Edward stood silently regarding the small gray man. Was it only a year and a half ago that he had been his tutor? It seemed so far in the past. Then he had been but a child, not yet seven. Now he was a king, going on nine.

Father John opened his eyes and saw Edward. He smiled his welcome as he got up from his knees. "Edward, I will not call you 'majesty' until the day that you are crowned. It is good to see you. The days were long without you."

"I have missed you, Father John," smiled Edward. "I would ask, think you there are any who could tutor such an one as Athelstain?"

"Is the young prince not perfect?"

"You know he is not."

"Yes, I know. And I know it to be costly for any to dare criticize the child within earshot of his mother."

"Athelstain has some hearing if the noise be loud enough. After I had shouted at him he called me 'Bubba.' I think him not dimwitted, just deafened."

Father John sighed deeply. "Edward, I will help the little one all I can. Our queen does show such spite to any who do suggest any course of action to her. Who can tell, she may regard any shouting at Athelstain as criticism of the child." He shook his head sadly,

Edward took him by the hand, "Don't be sad, Father John. Come and break your fast with the king."

Together they went to the great hall. The tables were ready, but no others were yet there.

Father John said, "Edward, you ask me to eat with the king."

"So I did," giggled Edward. "Me! My grandsire would have said 'us,' but I think that I'm a better 'me' than an 'us.' What think you?"

"I think you are still my playful knave! Don't let events change you too much, my son. Ah, here come the bread and sausages and ale."

During the week when the bishop was making his slow progress from York to Torr, preparations for Edward's coronation were going on feverishly. His robe was completed. The crown was brought from the royal treasury and tried on Edward's head. Being far too large, it promptly slipped down over the boy's eyes. When the crown was removed, it was taken to have a new cloth cap sewn inside.

King Alfred asked, "Lad, what happened when that crown was set upon your head?"

"I couldn't see."

"And you were not the first to be blinded by a crown. For many kings the crown is a blindfold which keeps them from seeing the true condition of their people and of their kingdoms. Other men often see the crown as a prize to be attained at all costs, and will break the laws of man and God to get that prize, never seeing their own grossness."

Edward looked confused. His grandfather smiled and said, "Fortunately, you have time to learn much before you must take on the full burden of being king. After the coronation we will select from among your nobles three who will manage the kingdom for you until you are of age."

"Will I yet live with you?"

"For a time. Your education is far from complete. How would you like to choose some companions to be students with you?"

"Men?"

"Nay. Boys like you. Sons of noble houses who can be your friends now and when you begin to rule, also."

"I am friends with lots of boys at Winchester."

"Sons of churls, and scullery boys, stable boys. They are not fit companions for a king."

"But I like them."

"For that, I am glad. A good king must like all levels of people and learn to judge them by their quality, not by their position. Nevertheless, you must have at least two boys who can be educated with you. You will find it much easier later on if you have some close friends. Even a king needs those he can trust and confide in."

"I don't know any of the sons of the nobles."

"What about your cousins, Earl Axel's boys?"

"Would they want to leave their home and live with me?"

"If that is what you desire. You are their king now. They are your subjects, to order as you will."

"And if in time I tire of them?"

"Then we will send them home and get you some new companions. Now, try on this linen shurte, if it be right for the coronation ceremony."

When King Alfred shook the folds from the garment, Edward grasped it by the hem. He looked closely at the complicated border and said, "My mother's weaving. None else could weave such. How can it be? I know this for her weaving. She made two such shurtes for my father, with this E and crown intertwined design. 'Twas said then that no other hands could weave so. Where did you get it, grandsire?"

"Karyl brought it. He had the garment made by a woman in one of the villages on his estates. Karyl's wife was a lady to your mother, was she not?"

Edward nodded, "She fell from the staircase and was killed."

"It must be that she had the secret of this pattern from your mother, and that she taught others to do it."

Edward agreed, "It must be so." He stroked the border with loving fingers. "The pattern is of my mother's design, created for my father, and now on a shurte for me, his son. If I can find that weaving woman, that design could be one future day on a shurte for my son."

"Try it on."

Edward quickly slipped off his tunic and pulled on the shurte.

"How does it appear? It feels as soft and pleasant as a benediction."

In the hedgerows around the fields of Swinstig the blackberries were turning dark and sweet. Rose went out at dawn with a basket to collect the berries before the birds and the village children pillaged the vines. Returning to the cottage, she set the berries to soak in cold water, while she made pastry shells and set them to bake on the griddle. Washing the berries free of dirt, leaves, and larvae, she set them to simmer in a pot, along with a measure of honey a peddler had brought to the door the day before. The berry tarts were completed, and cooling when Margrethe and Tammas came into the kitchen.

Rose said, "Berry tarts, my lady, made with the first of the hedge berries."

"Smell is good. Never anything smell better," declared Tammas.

"The aroma is enticing. Were these to eat now?"

"I made them for our evening meal."

"Please, one for Tammas now?" begged Tammas. Rose slipped a tart into his bowl. He ate it in tiny bites, savoring each crumb of the golden pastry, and wiping up the berry juice with a finger which he licked.

"Good. So good. Never eat anything so good." Tammas closed his eyes and sighed with pure pleasure. "Woman, you cook good. Best in world."

Rose's face flooded with color from the compliment, but she turned from him and said, "I've been doing my work. Now let's see some work from you. That garden has weeds waiting to meet the hoe."

Tammas went outside, grumbling to his work.

Margrethe said, "Rose, methinks the lad grows fond of you."

"He is fond of his belly."

"When you had gone to the funeral, Tammas worried about you for the entire time." Rose shrugged. Margrethe continued, "He is not an unlikely looking lad, now that he is well cared for."

"Mayhap not, But they say hereabouts, 'red of hair with dimpled chin, Devil always lurks within.' Tammas can look elsewhere for a woman."

However, when they gathered for the evening meal Rose welcomed Tammas with a smile. He gave her a startled grin. They consumed the bread and meat, and Rose set a berry tart before Tammas and before Margrethe. They spooned into them with delight. Tammas had almost consumed his when he looked up and said, "Rose, you not eat tart?"

She shook her head. "I made but three. You liked yours so much this morning that I gave you mine tonight." Tammas looked apologetic. "Tammas ate yours."

"I trow that is no great thing. I can bake more tarts on the morrow."

Tammas went out to look for a bit of wood for his carving. A bit to make something special for Rose.

In great pomp and with no haste at all, the bishop finally arrived at Torr Castle. His Reverence was more than a trifle annoyed to find the best suite of rooms in the King's Tower already occupied by two kings. With ill grace the bishop accepted more lowly accommodations. He wondered how he was expected to manage without a privy chamber of his own.

The bishop's servants were insufferably rude to the slovenly servants of the castle. This did nothing to promote harmony. Tensions grew with each passing hour, and it was plainly seen by all that it would be difficult to preserve even a modicum of peace for very long. Messengers were sent out to those of the nobles who were not already staying at the castle. The coronation would occur one day hence.

Edward awakened early on his coronation day. He was keyed to a feverish pitch of excitement. Thinking to calm the boy, King Alfred ordered him to drink strong wine instead of his usual ale for breakfast. The wine served to quiet Edward. He relaxed and let the harried preparations for his coronation flow around him.

Edward submitted to being scrubbed, then was dressed in a breech-clout, the new linen shurte, and his old tunic. He wore his old shoes, and old cloak. Mounted on his pony, riding at the back of the procession in company with Father John, Edward thought he looked dull as a hen sparrow. His grandfather, riding behind the bishop and his retainers, was splendid in his royal robes and crown. Like a scarlet cock in the fowl yard. The procession streaming behind were as colorfully attired as they could manage. Edward saw some as blue as jays, others as gold and brown as pheasants. What bird did Helene in her black put him in mind of? A rook, with her ladies around her like wrens.

The horses set a brisk pace. As they trotted along Edward sobered up and became aware of an urgent need.

"Father John, I need to go into the bushes."

"'Tis but a short time until we reach the church. Can you not wait?"

"No. I need to stop now."

"With all of this procession of nobles to know?"

"Better that, than for me to disgrace myself like an infant."

Edward turned his pony into the willows beside the road. In a few moments he was back, much relieved. Father John looked displeased, but, thought Edward, he would have looked even more displeased had Edward arrived at the church in wet clothing.

The bishop and his aides entered the church first. The nobles entered in the order of their rank and were seated with their ladies behind them. Helene and her ladies were seated near the sarcophagus of Ethelred. Minor officials and their wives sat next. All others who could squeeze into the church were there. The only ones to remain outside were Edward, Father John, King Alfred, and the armed guards.

The choir began their antiphonal chant of the *Benedictus* hymn. *"Benedictus qui venit in nomine Domini."* As their amen rolled out, King Alfred entered and was given a seat of honor on the dais.

Now all turned to gaze as Edward and Father John moved to the front of the chapel at a slow walk.

"I bring Edward, son of Ethelred Rex, to be crowned king of Wessex," intoned Father John firmly.

"Amen, amen, amen," responded the people.

Father John went out, leaving Edward standing alone.

The bishop arose. "Edward, born prince of this land, son of Ethelred Rex of Wessex, grandson of Alfred Rex of Sussex, do you come this day to become the anointed king?"

"I do," said Edward clearly.

"Do you uphold the laws of God and of man, placing honor above self, and truth above wealth?"

"I do."

"Will you pledge protection to the Holy Church and justice unto your subjects?"

"I will."

"We accept you to be anointed."

Two of the bishop's assistants removed Edward's tunic and had him slip off his shoes. Barefoot, and covered only by his shurte, Edward was led to the throne chair.

"In the name of the Father, Son, and Holy Spirit." The censer was swung around Edward, emitting great clouds of incense which caused Edward to sneeze.

"Aa-aa-aa-men," responded the clergy.

The bishop anointed Edward's forehead, the palms of his hands, and the soles of his feet with holy oil, while murmuring prayers rapidly in Latin.

Father John returned carrying the coronation robe and a pair of small boots. The purple robe was slipped over Edward's head, and the new red suede boots put on his feet. Edward's interest was centered on those magnificent boots. He wondered if Padraik, seated at the back of the church, could see these wonderful new boots. He hoped he could. He had to be reminded to hold his head up for the placing of the crown. A cloak of scarlet edged with miniver fur was pinned around his shoulders with a jeweled gold brooch. The royal scepter with its great golden orb was placed in his hands.

The choir chanted the *Te Deum*.

Edward sat painfully still for the remainder of the ceremony. He had no desire to cause the crown to slip or in any way to diminish the high dignity of his new title: Edward Rex, king of Wessex.

At the termination of the ceremony the scepter was taken by the bishop. Now the nobles came forward, one at a time to kneel before Edward and place both their hands between his. In this attitude they pledged their fealty to their new king, promising to defend and honor him. When they had given their oaths, they were free to leave the church. It seemed to Edward to be a very long time before they had all done so.

After this, the bishop addressed Edward, "And what is your will regarding Helene's relict of Ethelred?"

"She and her son are to find shelter under our roof so long as they desire."

The choir chanted the *Gloria Patria*, and the ceremony was at an end. King Alfred on one side, and Father John on the other led Edward from the church.

"Must I continue to wear this heavy crown?" asked Edward.

"For today, yes. Just as we wear ours," responded his grandfather.

Edward had difficulty in mounting his pony. The long robe and the cloak hampered him, and he was afraid that the crown might tilt. It was a tired, pale-faced boy-king, holding himself rigidly erect in his new dignity, who led the procession back to Torr Castle.

At the castle, the serfs and villeins had gathered. Oxen and pigs were being roasted over open fires in the tournament yard. Stacks of bread and barrels of beer and ale were set on tables. Now that the procession had returned the feasting could begin. There was food and drink for all to have their fill.

"Long live Edward, king of Wessex."

"And tomorrow," said King Alfred, "begins your royal progress through all of the villages of your land. All of the people must be allowed to see their new king."

CHAPTER 13

The royal progress for the newly crowned king was slow. Edward had expected to travel through his domain for two weeks at the most, but it was well over two months before the trip was completed. King Alfred had desired to speak privately with each of the nobles as the royal party passed through their villages. He sent his spies among the crowds of common folk to find their opinion of their lords. Based on his own observations and the reports of his spies, he selected three nobles who seemed to be best fitted to manage the affairs of the kingdom during Edward's minority. Their duties as the regent council would take but a portion of their time. The remainder of their time could be devoted to their own estates. Karyl was among the three chosen for the council. The other two were Geoffrey, on whose property Ethelred had been murdered, and Claud, who showed a great sense of justice for all men.

When the progress reached Dorchester, Axel and Gwynna seemed very pleased that their sons had been selected to be companions to the new king.

Edward spoke to his cousins Paul and Arthur, "When we came to visit you before, you cared not over much for us."

Arthur replied, "Verily, you were not the king, then."

Paul added, "And our sire says that we must always show a respect for those in authority over us. Else there be quarrelings and wars."

✢ ✢ ✢

The months slipped quickly past for Margrethe. One day as she and Rose were working together Margrethe asked, "How old be you now, Rose?"

"Seventeen at Midsummer Eve. My mother said she did so want to join in the St. John's bonfire night that her desire marked me with the firebrand."

"Do you not wish to marry soon?"

"Who would want one marked as I?"

"Anyone who knows you would. You will make a very good wife."

"Mayhap. Few bachelors look beyond this mark on my face."

"I know one who would: Tammas."

"Would I have him?"

"You could do far worse. Tammas would be a steady man."

"On unsteady legs! My lady, could we not go out now into the woods to seek out the plants which will yield dyes for our yarn?"

When Karyl stopped by the cottage for a visit he watched Rose closely. He said, "My lady, you have worked a miracle with that girl. When I first found her she was the abused, neglected child of an ignorant serf. She changed much whilst working in the kitchens of my manor house. Now you have made her to be clean, neat, and gentle of speech. She could well grace the household of a large landowner."

"I could have done nothing had Rose not had a good nature and a quick mind. She learns readily."

"Which makes me to wonder, could it be that you could teach other daughters of serfs to spin and weave and care for themselves? With none to teach them they grow but little better than the beasts in the field. Then they breed in ignorance and rear a litter as bestial as they are themselves. What think you of having a scole for the daughters of serfs?"

"Serfs only? Or would you include villeins?"

"Serfs have the greater need. Villeins pass their hearthside skills from mother to daughter."

"Methinks it would be a large undertaking. Such a scole would require a large hall and several workers to help us. Have you a place in readiness?"

"Nay. I did desire to speak first with you."

"What know I of keeping a scole?"

"You have ordered the affairs of a castle full of servants. You have the knowledge and the skill to make needlework and tapestries. You know methods of weaving which no others in this area do know. A serf's daughter who learned such things would have a chance not to spend her days grubbing in the fields and living in a sty like an animal. She could hope to find employment in the households of more prosperous villeins. Mayhap she could even sell her works to earn moneys for a dowry for herself."

"Would that we had time to think on this! Truth must be faced, my remaining sight is failing fast. If such a venture you desire, then it must be started now. Else there will be not time enough to teach what I do know."

Karyl made ready to depart, saying, "I shall search out a proper place for our scole. I will return in a sevenday."

"God keep you as you go."

"God be with you, who stay."

Geoffrey, Claud, and Karyl gathered every fortnight at Torr Castle to hold court for three days. They listened to petitions for redress from those who felt they had grievances against their neighbors. They adjucated boundary disputes between landowners, sentenced convicted miscreants, inspected the Crown lands to determine if they were well kept. They settled the questions of weregild, moneys paid to the survivors after the death of any man who met his end in service to his lord. For the serf, such payment was scarce enough to pay the gravedigger to bury him. For a villein, the compensation was four times the amount fixed for a serf. For a noble, the money was four times that of a villein.

There were also claims brought by the church to be settled. The church tax of a penny for every hearth, whether serf, villein, or noble, was always a cause for grievance.

Geoffrey grumbled, "Our estates must be as full of clergy spies as a hound is of fleas! How else could they know to the precise number how many peoples we have occupying what dwellings?"

Karyl replied, "The church has made use of informers, this we know. Peddlers are often paid by the church for such information. The people trust peddlers and are open with them about what they own. Were we to send a court official to make an inventory of our peoples the people would be afeared, and hide much. Further, the wandering friars who go about from place to place are often making a census of all the hamlets and villages. But for this ill we have no cure. We can but endure."

When first the council had met, Helene came to sit with them. With firm politeness she was asked to remove herself.

"But I am the queen," she protested.

"You *were* the queen. Now you are but the relict of a king, occupying your apartments in this castle at the will of King Edward."

In great anger, Helene stormed up the staircase to her rooms. Athelstain came running to her, and she gave him a slap that sent him tumbling in tears. Helene then grabbed up the unfortunate child, shaking him harshly while she screamed, "Why can't you be perfect? How am I to make a king of you?"

The nurse came running quickly to remove Athelstain from her. His face was bruised and his nose bloodied, but he had not suffered other physical harm.

Helene sent for Radnar. He came, saying, "Ah, now your majesty has payment ready for me!"

Which served to anger Helene the more. "How dare you expect payment for the honor of serving me?"

"Because you did so promise, and a wise queen honors her promises."

"Payment and reward were to be yours when you had cleared the path for Athelstain to be king."

"Until such time, your gentle majesty, would not a bit of moneys serve to cloak our plans in secrecy? Rash words often slip from lips not sealed with cash."

With ill grace Helene searched her small jewel casket and found some coins. "Take these, leech! Mayhap they will cause some new plans to hatch in your belly. How think you we can best make an attempt upon the life of the king?"

Karyl found a suitably large ville to be used as a scole. It had been let to shiftless villeins who tried to get by with little labor. Karyl had permitted their rents to owe for two years before evicting them. It was a good property with trees, tilled fields, and a brook running through the grazing meadow. There were stone and brick outbuildings for the cattle byre, pig sty and fowl house. The dwelling had a large central hall, with kitchen behind, flanked by two wings, each consisting of one large downstairs room, with two sleeping rooms above. This house was built of stone, with several small windows, at least two to each room. These small windows were set splayed into the thick stone walls to let in a maximum of light from a minimum of glass.

Karyl took Margrethe and Rose to see the house before making the commitment final. "Will it do?" he asked.

"Very well, if we have serfs to till the fields," replied Margrethe.

"And help for me," added Rose. "I cannot do all of kitchen and house work alone."

"What of Tammas?" asked Margrethe.

"He has no wife. I see no wisdom in having a single man living with a flock of young girls. 'Twould but lead to trouble," replied Karyl.

"Tammas would to court Rose, but she refuses him," said Margrethe.

"Is this true?" Karyl asked Rose.

"Yes. It be true." Rose looked glum.

"Then I will speak with the lad. If there be no hindrance I order you to marry Tammas."

Rose stifled her protests, but looked mutinous.

"Speak girl, what know you against Tammas?"

"Naught. I do but desire to remain with my lady. A husband is but a sore trial, my mother did say."

"Best you marry Tammas if he will have you. Men are all much the same. Be virtuous, cook well, and deny him not his bed. That keeps any man happy with a wife."

On the ride back to the cottage Rose wiped surreptitious tears with the hem of her sleeve. Tammas was standing in the cottage doorway awaiting them.

When the riders had alighted Karyl turned to Tammas, "Tammas, do you like Rose?"

Tammas blushed scarlet, started to deny it, then said "Yes. I do."

"Have you a desire for her to wife?"

"Yes. But that woman not want."

"Have you a wife in your country?"

"Tammas have nobody. All killed by Norsemen."

"Would you like to remain with the lady and Rose whilst they make a scole for to teach weaving and needlework?"

"Would stay ever."

"Then I so order it. You will take Rose to wife."

Tammas limped away to his room. He returned carrying something in his hand. "Make for you," he said, thrusting it into Rose's hands,

Rose looked at the gift. It was an exquisitely made heart, half as large as the palm of her hand. On the front of the heart a wild rose was carved, with a delicate surround of vine and leaves. On the back there was affixed a copper pin.

"Is for cloak. Look pretty."

"Oh Tammas," Rose was weeping openly now. "None ever gave me so beautiful a thing. You made this for me. Oh, Tammas!"

"Why that woman cry? Not like brooch?"

"She likes it very much." said Margrethe.

"It is the work of a craftsman. Where did you learn such?" asked Karyl.

"Mine father. He work so."

"I will pay you money to carve for me. I would to have some decorative carving done for my manor house."

"I leave the lady? Not like that."

"No. If it be your will, you and Rose will live with the lady as long as you desire."

"Happy! Tammas happy! Please, when I marry?"

"As soon as you and she agree. The three of us will be moving from this cottage next week."

The Viking ships had cruised within sight of the shore watchers all along the southern coast for several weeks. They made no threatening moves, just showing their presence day after day. English boats normally engaged in coastal trade remained in their ports. None cared to be food for the sea sharks of the Norse.

When the Norsemen did attack, it was with greater planning and more cunning than was normally shown by them. They had a new leader, Guthrum the Savage, grandson of the Guthrum who had sworn peace with King Alfred's father.

Guthrum the Savage led his forces in a landing at Porchester, coming in with the tide under the cover of the predawn darkness. The defenders of the shore fort were slain as they slept. The Viking ships were drawn for safekeeping within the walls of the fort. Then the Vikings divided into two groups, one striking north toward

Winchester, the other moving east toward Chichester. Each group was as ravenous as a pack of wolves in a lean winter, burning, looting, killing all of the people they encountered.

News of the invasion reached King Alfred, who rallied a troop at Winchester. Norsemen had been easily defeated by his soldiers in the past. He reckoned that thirty men would be more than enough to take care of these Vikings.

Edward, Paul, and Arthur begged to be allowed to go with the soldiers who were being sent to route the raiders. "Why can we not go, grandsire?" asked Edward. "We have learned our fighting lesson well. We practice every day with our swords, and we all can shoot the center of the targets from our galloping ponies."

"Have you yet killed a man?" asked King Alfred. "To battle the Norse is no light thing. Any warrior who fights them must not blanch at killing. Even a moment of hesitation is fatal. The Norse fight not like men, but like demons of death. You lads remain here in the castle. The seasoned warriors will seek and kill the invaders." He ordered the troop of thirty men to leave at once.

These thirty men, mounted on their heavy war horses, had ridden but a few leagues south when they could see the smoke rising from the building torched by the Norsemen. The soldiers spurred their horses on to greater speed.

The stone bridge at Twyford, with its three great arches, was said to have been built by the Romans. It was broad enough that four could ride abreast, and the soldiers' horses galloped onto it. From either end of the bridge the Norsemen ran at them. Vikings boiled up over the sides of the bridge where they had been hiding. The horses had no room to maneuver and panicked when they trampled warm bodies. The paving stones grew slippery with blood. The battle cries of the warriors, the screams of the dying, the clash of weapons, and frantic neighing of the steeds combined in horrid cacophony. The Norsemen killed the soldiers first, then slaughtered the horses. Leaving the bridge blocked with bodies, the Norse ran on to continue their murderous invasion. Some of their number had been left among the dead on the bridge, but of Alfred's men, not one was left alive.

There were none to carry the news of their deaths to Winchester.

Rose and Tammas were married at the small abbey in Newcross. Margrethe insisted on wrapping a wimple around Rose's head, framing her face in such a way that only a finger-width of the birthmark showed. Margrethe had made Rose the gift of a new sky-blue hood and cloak. Rose wore the brooch Tammas had made. She and Tammas looked like a gently born couple as they set out alone for the abbey.

Margrethe remained at the new scole. Karyl had said that he would bring the students this day. When Karyl did arrive, in a farm cart with seven little girls, Margrethe felt her doubts rising. The girls were sent indoors in the keeping of Lisel, the woman Karyl had assigned to aid Rose. Lisel and her man, Hals, were middle-aged and childless. They had worked as servants for a prosperous villein for many years.

Margrethe said to Karyl, "You said that you would bring six girls. Why be there seven?"

"That smallest girl is orphaned. The family she was living with no longer would keep her. She had no place to go and she fears everyone."

"Poor child. And she so young!"

"I think her rising eight, small because of being starved."

"Have you time to come in for refreshment with me?"

"Nay. I must needs go home and get my destrier and armor, and rally my fighting men. A call has come from your father for all of the soldiers we can muster. The Norsemen have landed in force. They threaten both Winchester and Chichester. They occupy the fort at Porchester. They have killed a troop of soldiers your father sent against them. Now they have so entrenched themselves that we will have much difficulty dislodging them."

"Think you there is danger to Edward?"

"Nay. The Norse could never take the castle at Winchester."

"Have a care for your safety, Karyl. I will pray for you."

"I shall return soon. This fighting will take but few days. These Norsemen are deadly and well supplied now from their raiding, but we are fighting for our land, and there will be many more of us than there are of them."

"Jesu guard you, and strengthen your arm."

CHAPTER 14

When the details for the scole were first being worked out, Karyl asked Margrethe, "What name shall you be called? To me you will ever be 'my lady,' but what will those who work on the scole properties call you? To use your given name could cause some to recall that we had a missing Queen Margrethe."

Margrethe thought a moment, then responded, "Padraik often said that a thing almost revealed is hidden best. When my brother William was a babe learning to speak, he called me Grethe. Mayhap I could become the Lady Grethe?"

"So shall you be. Few hereabouts ever saw you when you were queen. They will not be apt to recognize you at sight."

To the serfs who tilled the fields and cared for the animals, to Hals and Lisel, to the children at the scole Margrethe became the Lady Grethe. To Rose and Tammas, both now blooming with the happiness of their newly married estate she was still just "lady."

With Karyl gone to lead his men to Winchester to fight the Vikings, Margrethe planned the curriculum for the scole alone. She felt much the need to have someone to counsel and aid her in making decisions. When she had fretted over her choices for some time, the Lady Grethe would sigh and say, "If I be wrong there is no great harm done. The sun will not cease rising."

When the children, Lisabel, Anna, Therese, Celia, Katrine, Priscilla, and tiny Mara, had been given their first meal together, Lady Grethe spoke to them. "By the gracious will of Karyl, whose serfs ye be, this scole was established to teach you needlework, spinning, weaving, cooking, and other domestic arts. You will not work all the time. Each day there will be a time to play."

Priscilla, the largest and most outspoken of the group, asked, "Please, Lady Grethe, what do we when we play?"

"Do what it pleases you to do. Do nothing if you so desire. Go gather wildflowers in the meadow, or sit beside the brook and dabble in the water."

The children seemed totally at a loss. They mumbled to each other in low voices, trying to discover what play could be.

Rose said, "Lady, these children have worked from can see to can't see every day since they have been old enough to walk to the fields. They have never had time to play. Never learned any games. Know no songs. They only know work and dirt, hunger, fleas and lice, with harsh words and hard blows to cause them to work faster. Now you have fed them enough that their hunger is gone. I will take them out with me to remove their dirt and vermin. These have come upon a strange new way of living, and will need time to accustom to it."

The two gray kits helped much to fill up the time set aside for play. The girls could always sit and watch the antics of the two who were fast growing into young cattes.

At first little Mara showed great fear of the kits. When questioned she said, "They bite."

"No, they don't," replied Rose.

Mara displayed her thin arms, marked with white scars, "Dog bite."

"You be gentle with the kits, they will be gentle with you. If you harm them they will scratch you."

Gradually Mara brought herself to touch Gray Girl. "Soft. Warm." Gray Girl arched her back and rubbed against Mara's legs purring loudly. "It's growling."

"Nay, she's singing. She likes you."

Unwilling to be neglected, Gray Boy came to claim a share of Mara's attention for himself. Mara squatted, half-smiling, to stroke a kit with each hand.

The Norsemen had advanced to the outskirts of Winchester. They encircled the city with a thin ring of death. At no point in the circle were there many Norsemen. At no point were there none. They put the torch to the ripe fields of grain surrounding the city. They looted, destroyed, and killed at every nearby villa. No supplies could come into Winchester unless accompanied by a large troop of well-armed cavalry. If the soldiers rode at the alert, weapons in hand, the Norsemen melted into the forest. There they waited and watched, hoping for a straggler, or for a foolish band of merchants traveling without protection. Daily incidents occurred to fuel afresh the fear flames of rumor which swept through the countryside.

There had been signs and portents before the coming of these Norsemen. Strange comets had streaked across the heavens. In the forest devils and smaller demons had been seen. Glowing lights had flashed from the hilltops, and wild cries and booming sounds filled the night air. A two-headed calf was born at Wycliff.

The superstitious peasant folk had taken refuge in their religion. They consulted local witches and clairvoyants. All predicted doom and the end of the kingdom. If not immediately, there certainly by the year A.D. 1000. The Lord's time was now fulfilled. The world would end soon. The churches were full.

King Alfred had never felt the weight of his throne to be so oppressive as now. Winchester was full of fearful idle people who had fled to the city for safety, and now had little to do except spread rumors and promote despair. King Alfred would that word could come from Chichester. Had the Norsemen destroyed that city completely? Was their maneuver in that direction a feint, or had they determined to occupy the port of Chichester? Genuine news arrived infrequently, but a fresh supply of rumors was to be had each day. King Alfred spent more than his wonted time in reading the book of Psalms and prayers that he ever carried with him. If God heard his petitions, He did not answer.

It was a blackened landscape that Karyl and his recruits passed through on the way to Winchester. The burned-out ruins of manors and cottages stood like irregular tombstones over the dead land. Every dead body and burned field fed their hatred of the Norsemen. They could feel hostile eyes watching from the edge of the forests. That they reached Winchester in safety was due to their numbers and to the fact that the Norse had no great skill as bowmen.

Upon arriving at the castle Karyl requested an audience with King Alfred. When he was shown into the main hall, Karyl was surprised to see Edward and his companions seated near to the king.

"Part of their training in statecraft," explained Alfred. "In years to come it will be required of them to cope with the Norsemen, even as we must do now. They must learn these lessons well."

Karyl asked, "Where be the main body of the Norse now?"

"Nowhere, and everywhere. That Guthrum is clever. He split his force evenly, half this way, half to Chichester."

"No spies to carry word of their plans?"

"Nay. Would to God it were so that we could send our Padraik to gather information for us. As it stands, no true information comes in. Frightened villagers carry tales of atrocities to the city daily. Mostly just rumors, few solid facts."

"If it please your majesties, this is the plan which our council has devised for this time of crisis. Whilst I am here, Geoffrey and Claud will hold court together at Torr Castle. When I return, each of them will come in turn, with their troops to aid in this battle against the Vikings. Vikings are but mortal men, and can be slain. Every one which we destroy is one less to batten upon the countryside."

"They seem to know this well. They hide from our fighting men in thick brush where horses cannot go."

"Can they be seen?"

"They oft do show themselves as bait, to lure our men into ambush."

"Do they carry but their swords and axes as weapons?"

"Yes. Their throwing axes they can hurl a great distance with deadly accuracy. We have lost many men to those axes."

"Your majesty, the untamed Cymry have a weapon which could prove useful. They have a bow, a long bow, with twice the range and power of our bows. It is not a weapon to use from horseback, but with it men on foot could pick off these Norsemen at a greater distance than they could hurl their axes."

"How much time would it require to get some of these long bows?"

"That depends on if these wild warriors of Wales will agree to aid us against the Vikings. Our relations with Rhys ap Daffyd are not too hostile, are they?"

"Nay. We do some trade with his people. How soon, think you, we could get these long bows?"

"Straight distance it be thirty leagues to his castle. That would include crossing the Bristol waters by coracle. By road, it would be roughly forty leagues. Mayhap more."

"Time does not favor us. Eight leagues is a full day of riding hard with fresh horses. To go to the Cymry, get the long bows and return would take at least a fortnight. Is this weapon worth the time and effort it would take to obtain it?"

"Majesty, I have seen a shaft from a long bow pass all the way through a man. Such is their power."

"Then we empower you to take a well-armed troop and go quickly. Tell Padraik we desire him to go with you. He can speak the garbled tongue of the men of Wales."

Edward broke in, "Please, grandsire, let us and Paul and Arthur go with Karyl to Wales."

"Nay, you be too young to fight Vikings."

"Padraik is too old, yet he goes."

"Padraik has a useful tool, his gift of language. What could you add to the expedition except a hindrance?"

"Nothing, grandsire." Edward looked crestfallen.

"Mayhap when Karyl returns with this new style of bow you lads would do well to learn to use it."

"Oh yes, grandsire!" A sunshine smile swept over Edward's face. He and his companions went from the hall full of dreams of using the new bows. Little did they reckon that the six-foot-long bow made of stout yew, and much thicker in the body than their bows, would be impossible for their childish arms to pull.

For the most part, the summer weather was dry. Mornings dawned sweet with pale light and birdsong long before sunup. One such morn Rose awakened to a strange, half-strangled crow, a sound that she could not place. Slipping softly from the bed, not to awaken Tammas, she looked silently down from the window.

There, on the dew-wet grass, Mara and the kits were at play. Gray Boy would tap Mara's bare foot with his paw, then race away as she ran after him. Gray Girl would snatch up a dry grass stem, or a fallen leaf, and race after them. As the three romped together Mara made the strange sound again. Chasing in circles with the kits over the soft grass Mara was laughing, the first laughter of her life.

Each of the seven girls was given a square of woolen cloth and a quantity of brightly dyed yarn. Rose showed them how to thread their bone needles, and they were ready for their first lesson in needlework. Lady Grethe went from one to another, showing them by patient example how to stitch the yarn into large petaled flowers.

Internally, Lady Grethe marveled that any girls could be so maladroit. They maneuvered their yarn into wild patterns with impossibly twisted knots. All Margrethe permitted herself to say aloud was, "How original, how very unusual." Then she herself would stitch another floral sample on the cloth.

As the days passed the cloths were covered with the bright yarn patterns. With practice the girls gained better control of their needles. Rose showed them how to hem the squares of cloth, and they were complete.

"What be these, Rose?" asked Celia.

"Can you not tell?"

"Nay. Never saw such before."

"They be kerchiefs, coverings for the head. When the winds do blow and the cold weather comes you tie them over your heads, thus. Then your head and ears will be warm."

The girls tried on their kerchiefs, each being of the opinion that her own was best. They all agreed that it were a pity to have to wait until cold weather to use these, the only bright new apparel they had ever owned.

By making all haste, Karyl and his group returned from Wales twelve days after their departure from Winchester. Karyl brought two dozen of the new long bows and, more important, two Cymric bowyers. These large, dark-haired, taciturn men were skilled in the shaping of the springy, close grained yew wood. They had brought with them yew staves to be used in training King Alfred's bowyers in making these new bows.

All of the men who had made the trip to Wales were travel-stained and weary. Padraik was near exhaustion. Being now past fifty years of age, he lacked the endurance of the younger men. He was glad to get back to Small John. That donkey was getting old and had been deemed not strong or swift enough for the journey. Padraik patted and stroked the beast who nuzzled and snuffled at him. "Old friend, your white hairs are as numerous as mine. But yet we serve, we serve. Some there are who need us." Small John stamped his agreement.

The warriors gathered in the courtyard of Winchester Castle to see a demonstration of the new long bows. Karyl chose two men whom he knew to be superior archers and handed each an unstrung bow. These two attempted to brace the bows as they had their short bows, to no avail, Karyl motioned to the two Cymry to take the bows. They held them so that the heel of the bow rested across the left foot, tip to the ground, string to the front. They stepped through the bow with the right foot, and tightened the string by stretching it upward into the nocke whilst holding the bend of the bow firmly with the pressure of both legs, one behind and one before the yew body. The Cymry did this so quickly that it seemed but one fluid movement that they made.

The target butts had been set at the normal bow range. The Cymry called for Padraik. He listened to them a moment and said, "They request that the butts be set back another thirty yards."

"Thirty yards?"

"They do so request."

The courtyard was hushed as the target range was increased, and the bowmen took aim. They drew the strings back to their ears. As one, they let fly, both arrows finding the center of their target butts.

King Alfred asked, "Is their range greater still?"

Padraik translated the question, and the answer. "Yea. Range can be twice as far, but this is the limit for perfect accuracy and full power."

"Have them to show us more."

The bowyers each placed six more arrows beside the ones already in the butts.

King Alfred said, "Now if they will but train our bowmen, as well as our bowyers in the manufacture of such bows, all will be well."

The tournament yard was no safe place to be during the following week. Archers were there practicing with the new bows at all hours of daylight. They had to become adjusted to the greater weight of the draw, as well as to the longer arrows.

Together King Alfred and Karyl plotted to draw the Vikings from the woods.

"What think you, majesty, if my men and I go out in the guise of a band of merchants, with wagons laden with goods?"

"Men in the wagons, laden with long bows?"

"Yea. It should prove a most wholesome surprise for the Norsemen."

"We approve. Which men take you?"

"I would to take the ones who came with me. After we defeat the Norsemen we will go back to our homes. When I return to the court at Torr, Geoffrey and his men will come here. When they go home, they will be replaced by Claud and his men."

"So let it be."

Before dawn of the following day some of the fighting men who had accompanied Karyl to Winchester were dressed in the garb of merchants. Covered wagons were arranged into a caravan. Each wagon was filled with men armed with the new long bows.

This caravan exited from the city gate and set out on the road to the southwest. It moved at a sedate pace. From the woods the sound of a horn being wound came to them clearly.

Then the Norsemen came at a run, from both the right and left of the highroad, their war cries ululating on the air. The bowmen stepped from the wagons, and braced their long bows. The bowstrings twanged, and the arrows whistled as the first flight of arrows downed most of the Norsemen. A second flight took care of the rest. The action was finished in less than a trice.

The caravan moved on watchfully. Karyl had hoped to lure more Norse from their concealment, but there were no more along that section of the high road. They saw no more enemies on the journey home, for which Karyl was duly thankful.

Karyl went to his home manor to rest and hear from his stewards the reports on his fief before going to the court session at Torr. His fighting men joined him at Torr Castles thence to follow Geoffrey to his castellated manor. There, they taught the use of the long bow to Geoffrey's men. Karyl's warriors parted with the new weapons with reluctance, even though they realized full well that these long bows were all needed now in the struggle to dislodge the Norsemen.

Geoffrey took his men to Winchester in the same guise as Karyl had brought his out, looking like a band of plump defenseless merchants. They were attacked near to the gate of the city, but had no difficulty in killing off all of the Norsemen with their deadly new weapon.

CHAPTER 15

The long bow proved effective in breaking the siege of Winchester by the Norsemen. When over half of their number had been slain, Guthrum called his warriors to retreat. With the foe retreating, the soldiers of King Alfred set out for Chichester. They found that the Norsemen had withdrawn from that city also. They followed the Norsemen to the fortress of Porchester, which had been set alight. Fires still burned in some of the buildings. The Norsemen had destroyed everything of value which they could not carry off to their boats.

By burning the grain fields and destroying the granaries, the Norsemen had created a wide area of famine. King Alfred had to divert a portion of his troops to gathering grain from other parts of the kingdom. He more than half expected a quick return of the Norsemen. However, they had retreated to Cygnet Islet off the southern coast, a point where they had already cached food and weapons to provide for a wintering. The Norse built simple weatherproof huts on the island. Here they would survive the bitter winter weather in comfortable, if unsanitary, conditions. New reinforcements were expected to join them in the spring.

By the time that Karyl and his men were due to rotate again to Winchester, there was no real need for their presence. The peasants were sowing crops of vegetables, which they hoped to harvest before the autumn frosts burned the fields.

King Alfred had purchased animals from as far away as Mercia to ensure that there would be some meat for the winter. The Norsemen had destroyed the wild forest creatures as well as the domesticated stock. The kingdom had been wounded, but would recover.

✞ ✞ ✞

Karyl returned to Torr Castle on a Sabbath day. He went to the chapel, and found it empty. He searched for Father John and called for him, to no avail. Seeing a castle servitor near, Karyl asked, "Where be Father John?"

"God knows," came the reply as the servitor hurried away.

The next servant he encountered Karyl grasped firmly by the arm, and asked, "Where be Father John?" The servant went white with fear, as he replied, "She said we were not to tell."

"She? Helene?"

The servant nodded. Karyl released the man, and went in search of Helene. When he questioned her regarding Father John she replied, "The little cleric be somewhere about the castle."

"As regent on the council, I demand to know where."

"In the dungeon, if you must know."

"By what rights be he there? Whatever he has done, he had no trial by court."

"By my right to protect my child. Father John was monstrous cruel to Athelstain!"

"Father John is known to be a gentle patient man, ever tender with young children."

"He did much harm to Athelstain."

"Father John harmed him physically?"

"I found him screaming and yelling at my son."

"Did you see him strike the child?"

"Athelstain had bruises."

"For this you put a man in the dungeon?"

"One does not yell at a prince of the realm, nor strike him."

"Neither does one usurp the rights of the court. Have the cleric brought before the council. Release him now."

Helene stood mutinous.

Karyl continued, "Then I shall issue the order. You, madame, do stand in danger of replacing the cleric in his cell. You have acted against the laws of this land."

Helene began to weep, "I was but a mother protecting my innocent babe."

"Enough. Go away. I shall have the story from Father John."

When Father John was brought before the council he was too weak to stand. A settle was brought for him, and a cup of wine to strengthen him. His hair was all snow-white, or would have been had it not been for the dungeon filth on it. His robe was dirty and torn. His forearms bore long, red, festering scratches.

"Tell us now, if you can, how you came to this condition?"

Father John began in a shaking voice "When our young king was here for his coronation, he found that his small brother cannot hear well. In fact, Athelstain can only hear if one screams at him. Edward did request that I try to help Athelstain. Edward had much pity for the child. Knowing well the temper of Queen Helene, I did attempt to penetrate Athelstain's deafness only when she was not near. I was teaching the child the *Pater Noster*. I would scream a phrase, which Athelstain would repeat. He was learning it slowly, until Helene came upon us. She had me cast into the dungeon. That is all my story."

"How came you by the wounds upon your arms?" asked Karyl.

"Those I have because of my belly. It does still desire food and drink. None was given to me unless I reached out through the ventage hole to beg. Brave souls among the servants would bring me a crust, a bone with a little meat still clinging, a little water. Once even some wine. But to get these I had to reach out through the spikes set in the ventage. At first I could keep from injury, but as I did weaken it was difficult to avoid being cut by the spikes."

Karyl shuddered inwardly. He knew well the dungeon ventage holes with their eight spikes set two on each side of the hole, pointing toward the center. A grille would have been more kind. Karyl asked, "And had you any bed but straw?"

"There was no straw. By the grace of God the weather has been dry. The floor of the cell was cold and hard, but not wet."

"How long were you in that cell?"

"Mayhap a month. Mayhap more. Some days ran together and I lost count of time."

"I shall see that our king knows of this injustice to his cleric," said Karyl. "Do you feel able to confront Helene?"

Father John nodded. A servant was sent to fetch Helene and Athelstain.

Athelstain came hurrying up to Father John, then stopped, dismayed by the emaciated, dirty figure. Athelstain was sporting a large bruise on his forehead, which had turned green and yellow.

To this bruise Helene pointed, saying, "See the evidence for yourselves. The priest did this to my son."

"Woman, you lie!" said Karyl. "The priest has been in the dungeon for a month. That bruise is not more than a week old."

Helene replied, "The child is unfortunate. Always falling on stairs, or stumbling against doors."

"Or mayhap against the hand of his mother? You will not abuse this priest again. He is being removed from the castle and a full report of this matter will be delivered to our king."

Margrethe was pleased to have a visit from Karyl a few days later. He asked, "Would you have room for one more waif who needs a refuge?"

"Certes. Bring her in."

"It is no girl." Karyl led the cleric in. "You know this refugee well."

Margrethe stepped close to the priest. "Father John?"

"My queen! Still alive?"

"Thanks only to heaven, and the efforts of our good Karyl. What do you here?"

"Karyl took me from the dungeon where Helene had put me to die."

"The dungeon? It was never in use in all the time that Ethelred was king."

Karyl said, "Helene does exceed her authority. With the regent council at Torr only three days out of a fortnight, she has too much freedom. A greater restraint must be placed upon her."

"You are ever welcome here, Father John, but where you will bide I know not. Every room in this house is filled."

"Is there a place in the outbuildings?" asked Karyl.

"A room meant for the cowherd is vacant, as we yet have no swine. If the room be suitable for a priest is in doubt."

"My lady, that room will be heaven to him after the dungeon."

"Let me call Lisel, she can take him to the cowherd's room."

Father John closed his eyes and began to tremble.

"What ails him?"

"I wist not. He has had these spells since being in the dungeon."

"That Helene has gone too far, to so insult a servant of our sweet Lord. Here, Father, is Lisel. She will take you to the room we spoke of."

"Which one, Lady Grethe?"

"The one meant for a cowherd. Have we another empty?"

"Nay. I will see that this priest is made comfortable."

"Go with Lisel, Father John," ordered Karyl.

The priest obediently followed Lisel from the room.

"It will be sweet to have the comforts of the church again," said Margrethe.

"As for that, I can but hope that Father John recovers himself enough to serve the church once more. How does the scole?"

"Wouldst please you to see?"

"Yea."

"Then come." Margrethe led the way across the hall to a large room on the left where Rose was teaching. There sat the girls, each on a stool, learning to spin. The distaff held in the crook of their left arms as the left hand teased a bit of wool from it, while the right hand twisted and wound the yarn onto a spindle. Each small face was set in grim determination.

When the girls looked up to see Margrethe and Karyl, their decorum collapsed. Down went the distaffs and spindles to the floor, as the girls surrounded Karyl. They stood silent before Karyl until Celia nudged Priscilla.

"I am to say thank you for our scole." She reddened.

Karyl smiled. "What have you learned?"

"Pretty needlework. Please, Lady Grethe, can we bring our kerchiefs to show?"

Margrethe gave consent, and the girls scampered away to return quickly, each small head now covered by a gaudy kerchief.

Karyl made a great pretense of admiring each one. He said, "You look as gay as a flower garden in May."

The girls, well pleased, went to store away their finery.

"I fear they do yet lack much skill with the needle."

"They have made a beginning. They are wonderfully changed."

"Rose is a good teacher. Whatever I have taught her she can put into words which these children understand."

"And Rose and Tammas?"

"Are as foolish fond of one another as ever any couple."

"I will come back to visit soon. The Norsemen have but retreated to an isle. They will cause us more trouble in the spring. But for the nonce we are free of them."

"And Edward?"

"Well. Chafing because your father would not permit him to show his valor in battling the Vikings. I must leave you now, my lady."

"God smooth the path of your going."

The autumn came sharp with cold winds. Rain poured down for days on end in excessive quantities. It was as if the heavens had saved up their moisture all summer to deluge the earth in the fall. Streams ran swollen bank to bank, and bridges which had stood from Roman times were washed away. Swine and sheep drowned in low-lying fields. Swine, being canny beasts, headed for the tops of hills. Serfs followed their lead. Few serfs were lost to the waters, though many of their huts were swept away.

When the regent council met at Torr it was agreed that Helene deserved to be without the services of a cleric. She was warned to restrain herself. A seneschal, who had been in the employment of Claud, was established at the castle to regulate the running of the household. Under his care a bit of order began to emerge from the slipshod chaos Helene had permitted.

Christmas that year found no religious celebration at Torr Castle, only feasting and drinking. And plotting by Helene, who resented the restrictions placed on her by the regent council.

Christmastide at the scole was a time of busy preparations. Rose and Lisel demonstrated to the children the proper way to pluck and draw two geese, which were roasted with chestnut stuffing. They were given the task of cracking the nuts they had gathered, so that the nutmeats could be used in the holiday baking, The little girls were totally ignorant of any but the simplest cookery and were amazed to see such luxury in a kitchen.

On Christmas morn the household attended the first mass served by Father John since he came to live at the scole. It was held in the main hall of the scole. Because there was no altar boy, Margrethe sang the responses in her soft, sweet voice. The serfs, Rose and Tammas, Lisel and Hals, and the children were all the congregation. Father John began the mass very shakily, but gained strength and assurance as he went. His face was radiant with his love for the Lord as he finished.

✞ ✞ ✞

Christmas at Winchester had been a busy time for King Alfred. Parts of his kingdom were near to famine from the ravages of the Norsemen. Other areas were in the same plight because of the violent rains of autumn. Supplies had to be imported from other areas. There were fortifications to strengthen or rebuild, alliances to be sought with rulers of the kingdoms to the north, and a mandatory use of the long bow to be established among all of the military forces.

Paul and Arthur had gone to visit their parents for the holiday season. Edward, left alone, was perpetually seeking out his grandfather with a childish request. "Grandsire, we are almost ten years old now. It is not mete that a king of such an age must ride a pony. We think it wants dignity. Can there be a horse for us?"

To such requests King Alfred would say, "We will see," then promptly forget the issue when urgent matters of state were brought to his attention.

Edward would go complaining the Padraik, "Our grandsire gives us no thought at all."

"Is there a reason that he should? What do you to lighten the heavy burdens that occupy his thoughts?"

"Naught. But we do need a horse."

"In due time your grandfather will attend the matter. For now, play your lute with me. Mayhap twill please your grandfather to have some music after his evening meal. Let us play the Christmas ballad that you learned last week. Wrong fingering, Edward! Do it thusly."

The winter was peaceful enough. Paul and Arthur returned to continue their education with Edward. Prince William, the heir to King Alfred's throne, now turned nineteen, was sent to Chichester with the responsibility of easing the distress of the populace. Edward was glad to see his uncle go. He had learned to resent William in the early days of his fosterage and had found no reason to change that opinion.

On Edward's tenth birthday King Alfred sent for him. "Wouldst like to go for a ride with us, Edward?"

"Oh, yea."

"Then go prepare your mount. We shall meet you in the stable courtyard."

Edward hurried away to the stables. There was a horse in his pony's stall. Edward wondered at first if he had the wrong stall. He checked again. He was right. He led the horse into the light and examined it. A beautiful golden filly. New tack hung in the stall. When Edward had saddled and bridled the filly, he led her outside. His grandfather was waiting. "Well, Edward?"

"Oh, grandsire, she is perfect!"

"Her name is Golden Honey, and you must take care to make her feel at home here. Shall we ride?"

The day was heavy with sullen clouds, heavy mists, and chill winds, but as they were returning from their ride Edward said, "Thank you, grandsire, for this most beautiful day of my whole life!"

Caring for Golden Honey took all of Edward's free time. He talked of nothing but her perfection until Arthur and Paul became jealously dissatisfied with their ponies. They wheedled horses from their father, and the boys were friends again.

Prince William was doing good work in Chichester. The reports he sent back to Winchester showed a steady increase in stores of grain and other foodstuffs in the city. There was also a report of military preparedness for the anticipated spring attack of the Vikings.

✟ ✟ ✟

At the scole the students had done their first bits of weaving, simple blankets to fit their small beds. These were made of lumpy yarn of the girls' own spinning. They would do better spinning and weaving in the months and years to come, but never any of which they would be more proud.

While the girls were learning simple weaving, Margrethe was teaching more complicated patterns to Rose. "Would that you could read, Rose, then I could write the instructions and you could follow them."

"That I can never do, lady, so needs must be that you teach me by your speech, and your example."

"Thankful I am that you learn quickly. Now see how this web must be set? The pattern is in both the woof and the warp."

✟ ✟ ✟

During the month of March the Norsemen on Cygnet Isle were busy preparing to invade the mainland. Winter had been spent in careening their boats, strengthening rudders, repairing damaged oars. Sails were mended, and lines spliced. Weapons were sharpened. Proper sacrifices made to the great god Odin and his son, Thor. All was in readiness for the invasion by the first of April.

On a blustery April day that alternated sunshine and showers, the Norse invaded Bognor Regis. They shouted aloud with the joy of killing as they destroyed the life of every dog, pig, cow, horse, and human that they found. Some of the chickens escaped to the woods.

Guthrum reasoned that the defenders would anticipate that he would divide his men as he had before, into two groups of attackers. This would cause King Alfred to divide his forces, expecting to fight in two directions at once. Instead, he kept his men tightly grouped, striking forward from their landing point like a bronze spearhead.

He left his sixteen boats drawn up on the shore, well above any high tide, with only six men to guard them.

Prince William sent word to Winchester at once that the Norse were attacking. Then he held a council of his officers to plan a defense. The Norse had been beaten in their attack before, driven back to the shore, and had escaped in their boats. Some men on the council now suggested burning the boats. Prince William said, "Nay. To burn the boats would only turn the Norse berserker, and they would fight and slay Englishmen to their last breath. Now here is my plan, one which they will not anticipate."

Prince William outlined a plan which was novel to the council. He completed the session by saying, "Now go you every man to battle this menace. I and my men will make my plan to work."

William took with him a group of but a dozen warriors. They circled their horses wide around the area known to be infested by the Norse, and rode under cover of darkness to the point where the boats lay.

In the predawn darkness, before cock crow, they dismounted, picketed their horses in the woods, and crept up silently to the boats. Two of the Norsemen were standing guard, clearly outlined by the light of the small watch fire. The other four were sleeping.

Arrows from the long bows took the lives of the drowsy guards, but not before one screamed a warning. The four remaining Norsemen were immediately awake and on the attack. The English closed in, confident of their victory. A Norse throwing ax caught Prince William in the left shoulder, severing muscles, tendons, and bones. Two of his men pulled him to safety.

"Bind me tightly, that I not lose much blood," ordered William. "And get back to the plan. It must be made to work."

The four remaining Norsemen were quickly disposed of. Now the men could give their full attention to the boats. They holed each boat in a dozen places, cutting long slits in the planking. These slits they filled with mud, and rubbed smooth to become invisible when dry.

The ropes binding the sails to the masts were cleverly cut by working a bodkin tip inside, and cutting the inner fibers, leaving the outer fibers intact. The metal bolts holding the rudders to the sterns had their heads sheared off. Sails were unfurled and slashed, then refurled so that they showed no damage.

It was midmorning before all of the sabotage was completed. "Now bury the bodies," ordered Prince William. A storm of protest rose from his men. "Bury them, and quickly! Don't leave them to give warning of our visit. When we drive the Norse back to this landing point they will be too busy fighting and retreating to notice that their guards are missing."

When the guards were buried, and the earth smoothed over their graves to show no trace of digging, Prince William fell unconscious. His men took turns riding with the prince held before them on the saddle.

Making all haste possible, the men headed for Winchester. They were certain that the prince would die and desired to unite him with his father before he did. The constant jarring of the trotting horses caused the blood to seep freely through the bandages.

At Fareham, which they reached at sundown, the men got a light, two-wheeled cart, and made a bed in it for the dying prince. They drove all through the night, coming to the city gate of Winchester just as it was being opened for the day. The prince was yet breathing as they delivered him to the castle. The castle servitors took charge, and the exhausted men collapsed on the ground. They had not rested in thirty-six hours.

Prince William was carried to the infirmary. Within the hour, he died. King Alfred sat by the side of his son and held his hand until death came. Edward, Paul, Arthur, Padraik, the castle cleric, the tutor, and other household members crowded the infirmary to witness the death.

King Alfred closeted himself in his chambers to cope with his grief alone.

Edward invited Padraik to come to his chamber. There, the serious-faced boy asked, "Padraik, did I make William to be killed?"

"Never, lad. Why do you ask?"

"When I was a small boy and became very angry at anyone I would say 'I hate you and I want you to die!' My mother used to say 'Edward, you must not ill-wish anyone. Think how you would feel if they *should* die.' I hated William, and I wished he would go away and never come back. I was glad when he was sent to Chichester. And now he is dead. Oh, Padraik," Edward's face contorted as he began to sob, "I did hate William, and he did die."

"Hush, now hush," soothed Padraik, taking the boy in his arms.

His voice muffled against Padraik's shoulder, Edward said, "I didn't really mean him to die. I feel terrible."

Padraik held the child until he sobbed himself Into exhaustion.

King Alfred mourned for a day. When evening had come he called for the men who had brought William to Chichester.

Refreshed physically by a day of sleeping, the men were yet numbed mentally by the loss of their prince. They responded as best they could to King Alfred's questions regarding William's plot to sabotage the Norse.

"He plotted well. Let the defeat of these Norsemen be his memorial. We will ride to the battle on the morrow. You men shall lead our troops and have the honor of striking the first blows to avenge your prince."

They rode all the next day without sighting the Norsemen. They encamped for the night, and as the darkness deepened the sentries could see far to the south the glow of fires set by the Norsemen.

The following morn King Alfred arranged his troops into the shape of a bow, with the tips pointing forward. It was wide enough to completely surround the spearhead formation of the Vikings.

As soon as the battle was joined, Guthrum perceived the danger and had the horns wind a retreat. Being on foot, his followers could not retreat as fast as Alfred's cavalry could advance. Some men had to be sacrificed to stand and die while the others made good their escape to the boats.

The boats were thrust out into the water, and the men climbed aboard. Chilled to the waist by the sea water, they eagerly set their oars and bent themselves to the task of moving their craft away from the shore and the deadly long bows.

The slits in the planking began leaking immediately. A quickening breeze came up, and the sails were unfurled, in all their ruined state. Yet they gave some assistance from wind as long as their damaged ropes held. Outside the shelter of the harbor, the heavy ocean swells caught against the rudders. Gradually the sheared bolts worked loose, and the rudders were inoperable.

The boats settled lower and lower in the water. Now the Norse shipped their oars and began their death chant. Chanting, they sank to meet their death. Death, the one thing which they had so freely dealt to others.

CHAPTER 16

The retreat of the Norsemen and the sinking of their boats would have been cause for celebration throughout the land, had Prince William not been slain. There was no royal procession for his funeral, as there would have been had he been king. The prince had been popular with the townsfolk, and they followed his cortege to Winchester Cathedral.

Prince William was entombed in a plain sarcophagus, one without an effigy on the lid. It bore the simple legend, "William, son of Alfred Rex," and the dates of birth and death.

King Alfred had turned his attention to repairing the havoc left by the invaders of his land. He dispatched Padraik to carry the news of her brother's death to Margrethe.

"And do you also to bring us report of the true conditions at Torr Castle," he commanded Padraik. "We like it not that we permitted ourselves to be swayed by the request of a child to give Helene and her son leave to reside there. She is evil enough to work deep mischief, like the poison in an old arrow wound. We should have made the two kingdoms of Wessex and Sussex into one when Ethelred died. At that time our daughter pleaded to have a kingdom for Edward to inherit. Now he is heir to our throne also. We have much to decide. You may go."

"Do I go swiftly, or no?"

"Go as you will. Look over the land. Report if aught seems amiss to you. Have you moneys for the journey?"

Padraik displayed a small pigskin moneybag, which was stuffed with coins. Bidding his master farewell, Padraik went to prepare Small John for the trip. Padraik had long been of the opinion that Small John understood perfectly that which he heard. Now as they proceeded on the high road southwest to Torr, Padraik explained everything to Small John. The donkey kept up his part of the conversation by moving his ears, forward, back, singly, together. He snorted and whickered at appropriate times, taking care not to interrupt.

Soon the steady rhythm of the hooves on the paving stones lured Padraik to change his flow of words for song. He extemporized as they went, singing of the early spring and the calling of the birds in the bare branches of the forest trees. He sang of the plowmen and their teams working in the fields, followed by the sowers broadcasting grain from their bright yellow aprons. Maidens with their skirts pinned high to keep them above the muck were working in the farmyards; they smiled and waved to Padraik, who made them part of his song. Cattle and swine, dogs and children trailing at the heels of their parents all were subjects of song for him. Had it not been for the sorrowful news he carried to Margrethe, he would have felt a perfect satisfaction with the journey.

The high road was busy with traffic, wagons from farms, carts of goods belonging to town merchants; peddlers traveling alone, some on foot, some on scraggy ponies; mounted soldiers; a few mendicant barefoot friars looking much like robbers; and once a group of ladies wearing heavy traveling gowns, mantled and wimpled until nothing of their flesh did show except their sweet, fresh faces. These ladies were in the care of a grim-visaged knight who looked sternly in all directions as they rode. The ladies giggled and chattered together, and greeted Padraik as Small John trotted briskly past their sedately walking horses.

Padraik's thoughts became more solemn as he recalled how lovely and vivacious Margrethe had been as a girl. He knew that she now had a scole, but knew not where it was located. By good chance Karyl was at his manor when Padraik arrived.

Padraik told him of King Alfred's desire for a true report on conditions at Torr Castle. Such report Karyl promised to have ready for Padraik to carry back with him on his return to Winchester. Karyl gave him instructions on how to find the scole.

He arrived late in the day at the scole, having taken the wrong lanes twice. Lisel answered to his rapping, and Padraik thought he had arrived at the wrong place until he saw Rose. He called out, and Rose hurried to him.

"Come in, Padraik, you are ever welcome! Lisel, go to fetch the lady."

Margrethe came and took Padraik by the hands, "I know that you bear ill news. It has sat heavy upon my heart all this day and for many days past. I have felt the shadow of death surrounding my childhood home. Who has died? Was it my father?"

"Nay, my lady, your brother William."

"William? But it cannot be. He is so much younger than I. What happened?"

"Death came for him on the blade of a Norse throwing ax. His men brought him to Winchester, where he died in company of your father."

"William! How could it be William? That round-eyed babe I held on my knees. Rose, come with me to my chamber. It is not good that the girls should see my grief."

Her tears began before Rose walked with her from the room.

Padraik went outside to take Small John to the outbuildings. On the way he saw a familiar figure. He called out, "Father John! What do you here?"

Startled, Father John went into one of his trembling fits. The spell passed quickly, and he said, "I serve our good queen, Margrethe. Helene considered a dungeon to be a fit abode for a cleric. Karyl rescued me and brought me here. What do you here?"

"I came to bring sad news of the death of William, brother to Margrethe."

"God rest his soul. I knew him not. He did never come to Torr."

"Nay. He was at his fosterage whilst our lady was queen. Now the Norsemen have killed him."

Small John stamped impatiently.

"Where can I stable my beast?"

"Mayhap where the swine should be. We have none yet. I sleep in the cowherd's room."

As they started for the cowshed the pupils saw them. It was their playtime, and they came running to surround Padraik and his donkey. Small John patiently endured being patted by little hands, which also stroked his neck and examined his mane. The girls chattered like starlings.

"Nice donkey."

"Does he bite?"

"Is he old? He's all gray."

"Can we ride him?"

"Pretty eyes!"

"What carries he in that case?"

"Is he hungered?"

Padraik replied, "He could well be hungered. Wist you where there could be an apple or a carrot for him?"

The girls rushed away to beg Lisel for apples and carrots. Padraik stabled Small John in the cowshed. His own small bag of clothes and the lute case he carried into the house. Lisel found a bit of food for him, also.

After Padraik had eaten, and cleansed himself of the dust of travel, he took his lute case to the main hall. Finding a settle to his liking, he sat and adjusted the tuning of the instrument.

Then Padraik gave the only gift he had to give to the sorrowing Margrethe. He filled the house with his music. The girls, charmed by the sounds of melody, came to sit on the floor near him. Padraik played and sang of death and sorrow, of hope and endurance. He sang of consolation, of the comfort of faith, and the enduring care of heaven. He concluded his concert with a hymn that Margrethe had always loved. Then he put his lute back in its case, as the little girls sat silent, entranced by the sounds they had heard, and the twilight deepened into night.

✢ ✢ ✢

Two years passed before Padraik's music was heard again at the scole, years that passed rapidly for the students. The girls had become expert at weaving and spinning, could do fine stitching, fair broidery, and make simple lace. Bolts of cloth of their manufacture began to accumulate until Karyl knew not what to do with it. He had no intention of setting up as a merchant.

For Margrethe the two years passed slowly. She counted the days and weeks from the time of the news of William's death. "Three days now, since I had the news." "Two months since Padraik came with the news." Twelve weeks, six months, a year, passed in this fashion. Then the hurt was not so sharp. There would always be some pain from losing William, for Margrethe had been more mother to him than sister. By the end of the second year Margrethe could speak of William without tears in her eyes or a lump of aching in her throat.

One day Margrethe awakened in darkness. The cocks had long since crowed. The bustle and noise in the house told of the occupants beginning their new day. Margrethe's first thought was "Why are they all up so early, when it is yet dark night?" Then the realization came as a thunderclap. She would always see only darkness now. For her there would never be a dawn. Only the deep night of total blindness. Margrethe went to the door of her chamber and called for Rose.

"Rose, the day which we knew would come is here. I can no longer see."

"Oh, lady! No!"

"Hush Rose. Do make no outcry. Why upset the children? I have plans ready for this day. When we divided the large room to the left of the great hall to make a room for the cleric, and a store room for the woven materials, I had this day in mind. Now I would to have the storage room as my chamber, so that I will not have to climb the stairs in darkness. This room can become the storage room. Is Tammas here this day, or does he work at the manor for Karyl?"

"He is here, lady."

"Please to send him to me. I will require a walking stick to my specification. Firstly, though, supervise me as I ready myself for the day. You must be my mirror now, to show me when I have a smudge on my nose, or my hair is untidy."

Margrethe worked quickly until she was ready to put on her gown. "I would to wear the blue one today, Rose. Please select it for me. We must mark each gown in some manner, so that my fingers can identify them. Now am I neat for the day?"

"Yea. You look no different than yesterday."

"That is good. Now, take the silver mirror from my small table there, I desire you to have it."

"Lady, it be too fine for me."

"Nonsense! You are fine as any lady of this land. It is not an object which I can ever use again. Having that mirror when I cannot use it is foolish. Your eyes are clear, Rose, you can enjoy it."

"My thanks, lady. I will send Tammas up now."

When Tammas came, Margrethe said, "Tammas, my blindness is now total. I have need that you make me a walking stick."

"Will this serve, lady?" asked Tammas, placing in her hands a polished walking stick with an elegant head, curved and carved like the head of a swan.

"It be beautiful, Tammas! How came you to have it?" Margrethe asked, running her fingers over the carving.

"I made it ready against this day many months ago."

"It fits me perfectly. Did Rose say that I do desire to move into the storage room downstairs?"

"Yea. Hals and I will care for the matter whilst you go to break your fast."

With her head held proudly erect, Margrethe, using her new walking stick, went downstairs to begin her first day in total darkness.

During this two-year period King Alfred had discovered a boat designer with a novel idea. This designer had made models of ships to demonstrate his theory that warships of twice the present length were highly feasible. With a change in the manner of stepping the masts, a more efficient use of the sails could possibly double the speed of these long boats. King Alfred was convinced by the models and ordered a group of six full-sized craft to be built for his navy. If these six proved satisfactory, then all of the old naval craft would be replaced by the new design.

While the ships were being built, King Alfred turned his attention to reorganizing the army, and simplifying its structure. When satisfied with the changes in the army, he turned to a major overhaul of the civil law. He kept teams of investigators busy collecting the various local laws from all over his kingdom. These were carefully examined and evaluated as to their degree of justice and efficacy. The ones which passed the severe scrutiny of the council and King Alfred were incorporated into one great uniform code of law that would apply to the entire kingdom.

Alfred yet pondered the question of what to do regarding the unification of Wessex and Sussex into one kingdom. Eventually it would have to be done. If he did not do it, then Edward must, as he would have both kingdoms to rule.

Shortly after Edward's twelfth birthday King Alfred decided to take his court to visit Torr Castle. He had not intended that Edward should go, but the lad begged to visit his old home again. In addition, Paul and Arthur desired to spend some time at their home in Dorchester. Paul and Arthur, being now fourteen and fifteen years old, were beginning to regard women with an interest that left Edward out. It seemed to Edward that they often forgot that he was their king, and they merely his second cousins. He would be happy to be without them for a time.

King Alfred sent advance couriers to prepare the castle for the arrival of his court. The court traveled at a moderate pace through snow slush, raw winds, sleet, and chill rains. It was with relief that they at last beheld Torr Castle brooding on its steep hill.

When he saw the ensigns of the two kings, the keeper opened the castle gates without challenge. It was a work of but a few moments to got the horses stabled and the men into the great hall of the castle. Great fires roared in fireplaces each large enough to roast a whole ox.

The seneschal installed by the council to manage the household of Torr was doing a credible job. The cobwebs had been cleared away, the worst of the litter raked from the rushes on the floors. The servants now moved with reasonable alacrity.

Helene had been absent from the dining tables, as had Athelstain. Edward requested that his half-brother be brought to him. Helene and Athelstain came together. The boy, now five years old, was pale and sluggish, grossly overweight. He did not really remember Edward, but came to him willingly at his beckoning. Edward pulled him near, and shouted in his ear, "Greetings, brother Athelstain."

A look of delight and recognition came over Athelstain's fat face as he said, "Bubba! Bubba!" He sat down near Edward and refused to be budged.

Early next morn Athelstain found his way to Edward's chamber, calling, "Bubba, Bubba." Edward was torn between pity for the child and annoyance at having to endure his company. When he told his grandfather of the problem, his grandfather said, "Take the boy to ride."

Edward had a servant fetch the child's warm cloak and led him to the stables. When he inquired as to the whereabouts of Athelstain's pony, he was told the boy had no pony.

"But I sent him a pony myself, last year for his birthday. Where is it?"

"Mayhap the queen would know, or the seneschal. I be but new here," replied the stable master.

"What does Athelstain ride?"

"He never does."

"Is there anything here that he could ride?"

"An old mare, fat as he is. She's over here."

The dusty-black fat mare was not tall, indeed not much larger than a pony. Edward ordered it saddled. The stablemaster helped Athelstain mount. As Edward led the mare out of the stables it was plain that the boy knew not whether to shout with delight or shriek with fear.

Athelstain sat the mare well. He gained confidence as Edward led the beast around the courtyard. "Me," he said, reaching for the reins. Edward placed them cautiously in his hands. The mare did not move. Athelstain sat, unknowing. He had never heard the sounds that horsemen make to their mounts. Edward showed him how to nudge the mare with his heels, while giving a slap with the reins. The old mare began to move slowly, at an ambling walk. Athelstain glowed with pride. He was riding! Really riding!

Edward walked beside the mare and showed the boy how to turn his mount by guiding her with the reins. When he judged this first lesson to be long enough, Edward led the mare by the halter back into her stall.

Athelstain slid from the mare and clutched Edward around the waist. His hug and his grin served to make his meaning clear. He was highly animated returning to the castle hall, and his normally pasty cheeks had a touch of color.

Helene was in the great hall. Edward approached her saying, "Madame, where is the pony we sent our brother on his birthday last year?"

"'Twas a sickly beast! It died. I did never let Athelstain near it."

"It is our will that our brother have a pony and learn to ride well. We will appoint a riding master to see that he is well taught. Ponies sicken, that is true. Should another do so, we will send yet another." Edward looked at Helene with a hard expression, which she had often seen on the face of his father.

Each morn of the royal visit Edward went to the stables with Athelstain. He rode beside the child, around and around the courtyard for several days. One glorious morn Edward led the way to the castle gate, and Athelstain was outside of the castle walls for the first time in his life. Two grooms followed them discreetly.

Edward saw that the child was too busy drinking in all of the sights of the village to pay any attention to his horse. Edward reached for the rein and guided the horse to the open meadows at the edge of town. Here he gave Golden Honey freedom to run as she would. She worked off her excess of high spirits, and then came trotting back to Athelstain.

Athelstain nudged his mare into a trot, and looked amazed at the speed he was traveling. Another nudge brought more speed, but a short gallop was all the old black mare could manage. She was blowing hard and wheezing as they returned to the castle.

Athelstain looked a different child now than when Edward had first arrived. Now his skin was lightly tanned by the daily exposure to the elements. His cheeks had color, and his eyes were bright and alert.

Edward delivered Athelstain back to his mother and asked, "Has this child no tutor?"

"He is yet a babe!"

"He is past five years old. It is our will that a tutor be found for him, he hath much need of teaching. We will check on his progress."

"You would force the child too hard!"

"Nay. No fear. He is our father's son, and has much of his mulish nature. We go now to find our grandsire."

King Alfred was in consultation with Karyl, Claud, and Geoffrey. He motioned to Edward to wait outside the chamber. The conference ended soon, and Karyl remained behind to speak confidentially with King Alfred.

"Majesty, Margrethe now lives in total darkness. Her sight did fail completely last month. She does much desire that Padraik make a visit to her. She would also like a lute of her own. Music will aid her in enduring her blindness."

"Poor daughter! We are angered afresh at the one who caused this tragedy. She shall have Padraik, and a lute, and aught else that she does desire. How does she live?"

"On the whole, very well. The affairs of the scole demand much attention. She keeps her hands busy, and makes no great thing of being blind."

CHAPTER 17

Life improved dramatically for Athelstain after the tutor and the riding master appointed by Edward arrived at Torr Castle. Edward had also sent another pony, a sturdy gelding, brown with a white blaze. Athelstain insisted on riding every day that was not too stormy. He showed as great a love for riding as had his father.

The tutor was a patient, deep-voiced man, whose vibrant tones were easy for Athelstain to hear. When the tutor had started the task of teaching the boy he had no high hopes of success. He discovered that the boy had a quick mind, which had been as starved as his body had been overfed. Athelstain began to read and write. He spoke with the loud, toneless voice of the deaf, but he was speaking.

Helene vacillated between annoyance of what she regarded as Edward's interference in the manner in which her son was reared and relief to find that the boy had a bright mind. Mayhap she could yet push him onto the throne.

Padraik had to travel to Lewes to purchase the lute he wanted for Margrethe. A monk in the priory there was a superior craftsman of musical instruments. Padraik selected a golden lute with a fine grain to the wood pattern.

True, she could not see it, but mayhap the beauty of the instrument would communicate itself through her fingers.

Padraik's journey to the scole to carry the gift of the lute was not joyous, although he now rode Small John through pleasant early summer days. Padraik recalled the days when he had first joined the service of King Alfred. They had both been young men then of three and twenty. Margrethe had been a babe of one year only. She had charmed Padraik's heart from the first moment he saw her, and he had always held her dear as if she had been his own daughter. When she was learning to walk, many of her first steps were made clinging to Padraik's finger. His music had been her lullabies.

As Margrethe grew, she turned to Padraik with her small hurts. He had soothed, petted, comforted, and, if the occasion warranted, reprimanded her. Her mother, Athelfraida, had provided a good governess for the child. But she much preferred Padraik's company. She slipped away to be with him whenever she could.

Margrethe had been ten years old when her mother died giving birth to William. The newborn William had been swaddled and laid on Margrethe's lap for her to attend while the midwives tried in vain to staunch the hemorrhages that quickly killed their queen.

William thrived on the milk of his healthy young wet nurse. His nursery maids cared for him well, but Margrethe was certain that they did so only because of her supervision. She spent all her waking hours in a state of concern for baby William. Her small face grew pinched with her worries over the infant. She was trying to assume the role of mother to her baby brother and lacked the maturity to handle it.

King Alfred had been at that time much occupied with settling disputes over the borders with his neighbors to the north. He had not noticed a change in his daughter. When Padraik called his attention to Margrethe, he studied her thoughtfully.

"Poor poppet! To become a mother while yet a child herself. Better for her to go away from home for a time," said King Alfred.

In his mind's eye now, Padraik could see again the shocked disbelief on Margrethe's face when she was told that she would go to be schooled by the Benedictine nuns. "But what then will become of my baby?" she asked piteously.

"Your brother will be nurtured most carefully and faithfully by his nurses. Glad we are that you love him. The time has now come for you to go away and learn the things you must know to be a good queen one day. Had your mother lived she could have taught you, for she was ever a perfect wife."

Margrethe had thought that she could never bear to be away from baby William, but the abbess in charge of the Benedictine convent was so warmly loving that it eased her heart.

Padraik chuckled to himself when recalling the first holiday visit of Margrethe to her home. She had hastened to the nursery and reached for William. He had screamed with fright and clung to his nurse. William had forgotten her. Margrethe was hurt, but she gradually managed to make friends with the baby before returning to the convent.

At sixteen Margrethe was sent home, her education complete. She was capable and well trained, and would be an exceptional queen for any king. Her quick wit and peals of laughter brought fresh sunshine in King Alfred's life. She had always been full of high spirits and merry pranks, even to the extent of sometimes irritating others. She exclaimed with delight over little things, and made the givers of small gifts feel that they had given much. She could make a joke of the most awkward situation, and her laughter would lead others to laugh with her.

Padraik's thoughts became gloomy as he tried to probe the reason that such a golden maiden had come to her present sad state. His musing was broken when Small John ceased to walk. Padraik looked up, startled, to find himself in the courtyard of the inn where they normally stopped for the night when traveling this highroad. Padraik patted Small John on the neck, saying, "Wise little beast! You had your thoughts upon this journey, whilst mine did journey into the past. Faithful companion, you deserve the best this inn has to offer." To which Small John agreed.

When they arrived at the scole, they found themselves expected. "Lady said you be here today," reported Tammas as he opened the door to Padraik. He led Padraik to Margrethe's chamber. Padraik rapped at the door. A voice replied, "Come in, Padraik, and bring me my golden lute." He placed it into her hands. Margrethe ran her fingers over it, saying, "It is as I saw it." Feeling Padraik's confusion, Margrethe explained, "Now that my vision is gone, the pictures I see inside my mind grow very sharp. I can see when visitors will arrive. I can see when the children here at the scole do plot a mischief. I can see how conditions are all over this place, without moving from my chamber. I can see the location of lost objects." She laughed suddenly, "Methinks I can see more now than when I could see!"

Padraik said nothing. Margrethe continued, "Pray get your lute, and do you tune both instruments. Mayhap my fingers have not forgot their way over the strings."

As they played together, they found that Margrethe had forgotten some melodies. A few simple ones she recalled well. Of others, there were only fragments. After half an hour Margrethe called a halt.

"My fingers are sore and lame as Edward's were when you first began to teach him to play. How does my son?"

"He grows into a tall lad, tall as I be now. One day he behaves as a child, the next as a proper young king. This is a time of change for him, and uncertainty. For reason that his voice broke once as he sang, he now mislikes to sing before any. He plays very well."

"Padraik, I've had no one else for a confidant. I would to burden you with this. Karyl, son of Albert, has asked me to wife. What think you?"

"You could find no better man."

"Well do I know his worth. It is that I cherish him much that I am reluctant to saddle him with the burden of a blind wife."

"Are you not his burden now? And have been since the day that we saved you from murder?"

"Yea. This matter does much trouble my heart. A wife who is with him every day is more of a trial than is a dame who keeps a scole whom he visits not above twice in a month."

"More trial, mayhap, but also more reward. You could repay his years of loving care in the marriage bed."

Margrethe blushed scarlet to her hairline. "Padraik I had no such thoughts!"

"A certes you did, my lady, what else would wifing be?"

"To be his companion. As a wife it is possible I could become a mother again. I am not too old for that. Yea, you are right. I had thought of everything. Karyl be brave, and a true knight. Strong, and tender, with a compassion for all helpless things. Not given to drink or wenching. In all ways the man I would that Ethelred had been."

"Fortunate you are to have such a suitor."

"Yea. Padraik, could you do this favor for me? Speak of this matter with my father. I do much trust his wisdom."

Padraik remained with Margrethe for a month, during which her playing much improved.

Rose was now pregnant, proudly displaying her six-month swelling. The blackberries were ripe, and Margrethe set the girls to picking them during their playtime. Rose made blackberry tarts. When Rose served the tarts after the evening meal Tammas said, "Best I ever had. Woman, you best cook in whole world!" Rose and Tammas giggled over this, while the students looked puzzled.

Margrethe was reluctant to part with Padraik. "Have much care on your journey. I would that you could return soon. Bring me my father's word on Karyl's proposal."

"I will, my lady."

"God keep you safe, Padraik. My thanks for all of the comfort which you ever brought to my heart."

"God be with you, my lady."

Small John set out willingly on the return journey. Pleasantly warm sunshine with puff clouds for occasional shade made for comfortable traveling. They stopped by Karyl's manor to pick up a report he had prepared regarding the conditions at Torr Castle. Then they were off, back on the high road to Winchester.

A shadow swept across the road, causing Small John to shy. Padraik looked up to see a raven circling over them. It cawed three times, then flapped noisily away. Padraik felt a chill foreboding of evil. He quickly signed the cross over himself. Then, as there were no other travelers in sight, over Small John as well. Surely the Lord Jesu would love and protect a donkey also, as He, himself, and his sweet mother had ridden one. Sensing Padraik's apprehension Small John slowed his pace to a walk on a section of the road near Ringwood. Here, at the top of a rise, huge oak trees sheltered the road with their branches. And here, atop the largest branches which overhung the road, three murderous robbers lay in wait.

A blow from a cudgel felled Padraik, and another did the same for Small John. They lay stunned in the road.

"In ta bushes. In ta bushes," ordered the leader of the robbers. With some difficulty they dragged Padraik and Small John from the high road to the privacy of a bramble thicket where they had hollowed a retreat. Here they cut the throats of their victims.

"Get ta treasure chest from ta ass," ordered the leader. The lute case was unstrapped and opened. The robbers groaned in disappointment at the sight of the lute. One lifted a filthy hide-wrapped foot and stamped the shape of beauty from the lute. The other two laughed as the lute was smashed into splinters. Padraik's body was searched, and his pigskin bag of coins discovered.

"Siller and gole, all mine!" exclaimed on robber. "Na! Na! Divvy, or us takes yourn." They divided up the small pouch of coins, storing them in hiding places in their ragged garments. What could they buy with their sudden wealth? Food they could steal, but ale was hard to filch. Mayhap buy a cask of ale. Wenches! Coins would buy all kinds of wenches. They hastened toward the town and their dwelling hovel, minds fixed on the satisfactions of the flesh, no thought given to the lives and beauty they had just destroyed. They had killed so often over the years that murder was as natural to them as breathing. Killing was their livelihood.

When Padraik had been gone from Winchester for over two months, King Alfred sent a courier to Karyl with a message that Padraik was wanted for an important mission to Wales. The courier returned in a seven-day to report that Padraik had set out on his return journey a month before. No trace of him, or of Small John, had been glimpsed by the courier on the high road. He had gone missing, as lone travelers did far too often.

King Alfred cursed and swore when he realized that a tragic accident must have befallen Padraik. That his friend, servant, confidant had been killed he did not doubt. Where, along the way, he did not know. The incident served to strengthen his resolve to unite Wessex and Sussex into one kingdom and set up a system of guards along the roads to ensure greater safety to travelers.

It had been recorded that in Roman times travelers could go in safety on the roads all the way from Rome to London. The roads in southern Britain must become so again. If this would require the stationing of a garrison of troops at frequent intervals along the roads, as the Romans had done, then Alfred would do so.

He sorely missed Padraik. Padraik had been of more value in establishing of this kingdom than a hundred soldiers. With his gifts of music and language he could converse with and entertain foreign emissaries. He knew more state secrets than anyone except Alfred himself and had never told a one. His sharp eyes always saw whatever was amiss, and the common folk had spoken with him as they would among themselves. Thus could Padraik make true report of the needs and grievances of the people. Alfred sighed deeply. How could he ever replace Padraik? And why, of all times, did he have to get himself killed now, when he was so desperately needed to translate in the border dispute with the wild Cymry?

When next Karyl came to the scole, he spoke lightly of many things until Margrethe said, "Are you never going to talk with me of Padraik's death?"

"Why think you that he be dead?"

"I saw it happen. My heart felt his fear, and the pictures in my mind showed me what occurred. Padraik and Small John fell victim to rogues at the top of a rise where oak trees hang their branches out over the road. His bones, and those of Small John, lie hidden in a bramble thicket. I would to have Padraik decently interred. It is not right that wild beasts do scatter his bones."

"My lady saw which town was nearby?"

"Nay. That I saw not. Only the road with the rise overhung by the oaks."

"Do you recall the time of day when you saw the picturings?"

"Late in the afternoon. Near to the playtime for the girls. Why dost ask?"

"Padraik left my manor in early morn. He could have well been near Ringwood by the time he was struck down. There are several places there where the trees do overhang the road. My men shall search the thickets near them."

"My father would pay you well if you take Padraik's bones to Winchester."

"If we find aught, it shall be done. But not for pay. For respect of one who was honest and kind, and clever."

Margrethe brushed tears from her face as she said, "Oh, Karyl, how fortunate I am to have had love from two such men as Padraik and you."

It did not take many hours of searching for Karyl and his men to find the bodies of Small John and Padraik. Crows had picked the bones bare. Foxes had scattered them a bit. The ruins of the lute in the open case bore witness that these were the bodies they had sought.

Padraik's remains were gathered up along with the lute case and placed in a large wicker hamper for the trip to Winchester. Padraik was buried in holy ground at Winchester Cathedral.

King Alfred had been busy many months in the preparation for uniting Wessex and Sussex when Edward came to him one day looking perplexed. "Grandsire, if you become king of my kingdom, am I then a prince again?"

"Nay, lad. It will be only that your kingdom will have an unusual thing, two kings at the same time who are in harmony each with the other. Two kings in one kingdom does indicate war in most instances. We would that you were old enow to carry a part of the burden of the government."

"What would you have me to do?"

"Learn everything. Study everything. Every man can teach you something. Make every day yield you a profit of knowledge."

"I know as much as my tutor, now."

"If that be true, we will get another tutor. A king can never know enow."

"Think you that the peoples of our two kingdoms will agree happily as one kingdom?"

"We do. There has been peace between the two for so long, and they are all of the same stock. Not foreign like the Cymry or the Scots. Not outlanders, like the Danes. Peoples of one stock tend to think alike. And it is in thinking that a kingdom is ruled."

The two kingdoms were successfully united. King Alfred's great codex became the law of the land. The high roads were constantly patrolled now by soldiers. Travel was safer than at any time since the Romans had retreated from Britain. King Alfred doubled the size of his army. Twice as many men were now being well fed, well clothed, and trained to maintain the peace.

The trees and undergrowth along the highroads had been cut back to a distance of forty yards from the roadway. It prevented many ambushes. This work alone employed many men over the next three years.

By the time Edward reached the age of sixteen, his land was the best governed, most peaceful, most prosperous of any of the kingdoms of Britain.

CHAPTER 18

Rose was delivered of a girl. A midwife came from the village, and there were no complications. Tammas was delighted with the infant whose curls were bright copper. "Like mine sisters," he said, touching the little head gently with one finger.

"Very like your own hair," responded Rose.

"I can hold her?" Tammas asked, reaching for the babe.

Rose nodded. Tammas held his tiny daughter against his heart, murmuring to it in his Pictish tongue. He laid the babe back on the bed, in the curve of Rose's arm, and knelt beside the bed to kiss Rose.

"You be best wife in whole world."

Rose wept from the wave of warm happiness which swept through her.

Margrethe was glad to have an infant to tend. Tammas had made a cradle for the baby, carving a border of flowers on the hood. During the day the cradle was set in Margrethe's chamber. She rocked the cradle, crooned to the infant, and played for it the lullabies Padraik had played for her. She composed a simple melody, and set her own words to it for the baby.

> *Hush, hush, now sweetling,*
> *And close thine eyes,*
> *Hush, hush, sweet babe,*
> *Thy nurse is a queen.*

Father John baptized the infant, with Margrethe and Karyl as godparents. She was given Margrethe's name. The new little Margrethe, child of a serf, had a knight and a queen as her sponsors.

Gray Girl had produced her first litter of kits at the same time that little Rethe was born. She had born three females and one male. When Margrethe would sit, rocking, the cradle, Gray Girl would come carrying a kit in her mouth, and hop up onto Margrethe's lap to claim a share of attention. Gray Boy made no move to harm his young, but neither did he want them near him. In the next three years Gray Girl produced six more litters, totaling thirty kits in all. One pair the scole kept, the others were placed in good homes in the village. In a decade the area became famous for the fine gray-blue cattes, which later generations would consider to be native to the region.

Little Rethe was nearly three years old when she was replaced in the cradle by her newborn brother. Tammas was as proud of his son as any man could ever be. Andrew, he named the child; Andrew for his own father.

Freed from the work he had been doing on the regent council, Karyl could now devote more attention to the scole. He searched his fief to find any who knew aught of the brewing of dyes for the yarn. These he paid well to divulge their secrets. The students at the scole, under the guidance of Rose, made experiment with combinations of colors. By trial and error they learned to weave patterns of checks, stripes, and plaid.

The girls wove more than enough material for their own use, and supplied the needs of the servitors at Karyl's manor also. The surplus accumulated until Karyl settled on the idea of selling it to the cloth merchants. The moneys they paid Karyl divided into three parts, one to go to the scole, one to purchase more raw wool and flax, and one part to build up dowries for the girls.

"What think you, would it be wise to bring in more girls to train?" Karyl asked Margrethe.

"Yea. Mayhap two or three a year. The eldest of our girls will soon be leaving us for useful employment, or for marriage. It would be well to train others to replace them."

✥ ✥ ✥

Edward had not been to visit Torr Castle for over three years. Now he was planning a birthday surprise for Athelstain. From the reports the seneschal had sent, Edward knew how much Athelstain loved riding his pony. For the child's ninth birthday Edward planned to give him what he himself had most desired at that age—a horse. Perhaps even his own mare, Golden Honey.

For a year now Edward had been riding a splendid black destrier, a large, sleek stallion of rare intelligence. It had been trained for battle and taught to rear up and lash out with its front hooves at the enemy. It was trained to obey orders instantly. Edward felt both proud and confident when mounted on his stallion.

Now that he was near sixteen, Edward did much desire that his grandfather would permit him to engage in some of the border skirmishes. When Edward made such a request to his grandfather, King Alfred replied, "Edward. you know not what you ask. If we had Padraik we would have far fewer border skirmishes. Misunderstandings between peoples of differing tongues cause more fighting than does greed for gain or power. If everyone on this great isle of Britain spoke one tongue, we would have greater peace."

"When the Cymry slew the men whom you had sent to survey the location of a new road near to their border, why did you not fight?"

"Because we were fortunate enow to find an interpreter to go with us to the Cymry. There we found that their border guards had thought the road surveyors to be advance scouts for an invasion by us. Speaking together with their ruler we settled the matter peacefully. Why send more men to die for what was an error?"

"If we do not fight, men will call us craven."

"Think you that your grandsire is craven?"

"Nay. I know you to be honorable and brave. But other men will misdoubt your motives."

"Then so be it. The Lord Jesu, who is our light, said to forgive unto seventy times seven. Do we be wiser than He?"

Edward went away resentful. How could he get to show his valor, his skill in battle arts, and his wonderfully trained war-horse if every dispute was to be settled by talking? He took his destrier out for a gallop over the meadows outside the city. In his imagination he put the stallion at the foe, and slew them by the hundreds, thrusting with his lance, and hacking with his broadsword. After an hour Edward returned to the castle, fully convinced that King Alfred was wrong. Battle must be the ultimate in exciting sport!

Golden Honey had been in foal twice, and had thrown one very fine colt, which Edward had kept. Edward decided now to keep the colt for himself. It was a perfect replica of its mother in coloring. He would give Honey to Athelstain.

King Alfred was not pleased by this decision. The mare had been his own gift to Edward. "Why could you not give the colt to that boy?" he grumbled.

Edward went blithely forward with his plans. He dispatched a courier to Torr Castle, informing Athelstain that he would bring a special gift on his ninth birthday.

The boy was delighted, but Helene received the news sourly. She went into conference with Radnar.

"What think you we can do? Edward will be sixteen three weeks after Athelstain's birthday. At sixteen he will be co-regent with his grandsire over our land. Have we support enow among the folk to depose Edward and raise Athelstain to the throne?"

"Nay, my cherished queen, that I do misdoubt. The folk do like the new law under Alfred. They would give their loyalty to his grandson, rather than to Athelstain."

"Would that I had slain the brat when he was young and near at hand!"

"It be never too late for death. Alfred has no direct heirs other than Edward, has he?"

"None."

"Mayhap if Edward be dead, the folk could be persuaded that the son of their former king would be a better replacement for the aging Alfred than would a stranger."

"Mayhap. Let us think on this. Whatever we do must be done with all haste."

On his birthday Athelstain was up at dawn. His one thought was, "Today Brother Edward comes with my gift." The sun was scarce up when he insisted on going to await Edward's arrival at the gate to the inner courtyard. From here he had a clear view across the tournament yard to the main castle gateway. The hours dragged by more slowly than snails on a summer morn. Athelstain was just getting discouraged enough to consider returning to his chamber when he saw Edward, on his black destrier, followed by a mounted equerry who was leading a golden mare.

"Brother Edward!" shouted Athelstain, running toward the main gateway.

Edward dismounted and held out his arms to his brother.

After he had been warmly hugged, Athelstain asked, "Where is my present?" Edward turned and pointed to Golden Honey.

"She is for me?" asked Athelstain, "Is she really for me?" Edward nodded. He began patting and stroking the mare, using endearments in his loud, harsh voice. "She is beauty, my own beauty. Like sunshine. Like love."

Edward put his head close to Athelstain's and yelled, "Her name is Golden Honey."

"Thank you Edward! Thank you! I love her. I love you!"

"Have you a saddle for her?" yelled Edward.

"Yea. In the stables be many saddles."

"Go get her saddled, and we will ride."

Athelstain joyfully led the way toward the stables as Helene and Radnar emerged from the courtyard gate. Edward went to greet his father's relict.

"God give you good day."

"And to you. Would it please you to refresh yourself with some wine?" Helene asked, leading the way into the courtyard.

"That would be most pleasant," Edward smiled at Radnar, who was carrying a tray on which were three large wine cups filled with deep purple vintage. Edward continued, "Do you mind how our father used to say of us 'the boy has no stomach for wine at all'? Would that he could see us now. We can drink wine with the best."

Edward quaffed his entire cup without stopping. "Ah, delicious!"

Strange how numb his throat felt. A coldness spread into his limbs. Darkness closed down over his consciousness as he staggered and fell to the ground.

Helene said, "It would seem you still have no stomach for some wine."

Radnar asked, "How now? We must hide the body quickly. Athelstain will return from the stables soon."

"Hasten, and carry him to the courtyard well."

Helene raised the wooden well cover as Radnar dropped Edward's body into the well.

"My queen, you now do owe me much. We must choose a better hiding place on the morrow. I can hear Athelstain calling Edward now."

Helene hurried to the courtyard gate. Athelstain, now mounted on Golden Honey, had reined in beside Edward's destrier. He leaned down to hear what Helene shouted at him.

"Edward is unwell. He asks you go to ride in the east meadows, and he will join you later."

Athelstain and the equerry clattered away on their mounts.

That night two servitors returned late from the village, intent on entering the courtyard door of the castle. As they crossed the dark courtyard they became terrified, and ran quickly to the security of the castle. Teeth chattering with fear, they told their tale to the other servants.

"As we 'uns crossed near to the well, a blue light were dancing on the well cover!"

"Dids't stop to examine it?"

"Stop? Nay! When there be witchcraft about we don't linger."

"Would we had cleric in the castle. He could bless the well and send the devil away."

"There was nothing out there but two lack-wits who drank too much with their friends in the village," declared Thick Cathy, the fat cook.

"Woman, if you be so brave, go fetch some water from that well!"

"The scullery wench can go. I do not draw water."

The scullery maid picked up a pail with alacrity and marched bravely out the door as the other servants clustered in the doorway to watch. An owl called as she drew near to the well. A shaft of white rose from the well cover, then faded away as the dancing blue light appeared. The scullery maid dropped the pail and screamed with fright. She raced back to the doorway just as the other servants were closing the door. As she slipped inside the door was barred.

"Did you see?" she gasped. All affirmed that they had. Thick Cathy suggested, "We could tell the seneschal."

The seneschal! Fine thought. He could go out to deal with the spirits. They trooped in a group to locate the seneschal. He listened to their tale and said, "On the morrow we shall investigate the well. Nothing is accomplished by night except increased confusion. Now go to your beds, the lot of you. We will look into the well on the morrow." Happy to have rid themselves of the responsibility for solving the problem themselves, the servants went to bed.

None were brave enough to volunteer to search the well next morn. The seneschal, himself, had to raise the cover and peer into the well. He could see naught except the rough-hewn well stones lining the round shaft of the well. Only the stones, and the mosses and ferns which thrived in damp and darkness. The water level was hidden far down, in the dark. A bucket lowered into the water seemed to meet with an obstruction.

"Bring the grapnell," ordered the seneschal.

These giant four-pronged iron hooks, meant to catch on the stone abutments of fortress walls, were ideal for investigating the contents of the well. Attached to stout cable, they were dropped into the well. The first drag brought up only a piece torn from a tunic. The second cast hooked the body. It was brought up, streaming water, and laid on the cobbles.

A murmur of shocked dismay ran through the onlookers. The young king! How came he to be in the well?

Athelstain had been attracted by the activity and came out to see what was amiss. When he saw the water-logged body of Edward, he flung himself on it in a torment of grief, wailing from the depths of his soul.

The noise brought Helene, who called for the tutor to take Athelstain away to his chamber. It required two men to pry the boy away from the remains of his older brother.

Helene was both chagrined and angry that the body had been discovered. "Why is such being done?" she asked of the seneschal, indicating the men with the grapnells.

"Two servitors did see a blue light dancing on the well cover last night. A scullery maid went out to draw water and saw a shaft of white light as well as the dancing blue light, these were also seen by others. All of the servants were much affrighted and came to tell me. I promised to search the well this morn. Little did I think that the matter would prove aught of worth," the seneschal explained.

Helene shivered. Mayhap the saying was right, the murdered cannot rest without proper burial rites.

"Are you well?" inquired the seneschal.

"Nay. I be faint from the shock of seeing my dear stepson, our King Edward, lying dead." She feigned a weakness, leaning against the cold stone wall for support until her ladies came to conduct her to her chamber.

✣ ✣ ✣

Margrethe heard a light rapping on her chamber door. "Come," she said.

"Please, Lady Grethe, Rose sent me to ask if the young man is to be staying here for a time?" said Mara.

"What young man?"

"The young man that we saw enter your chamber. We were at our spinning, and through the open door we could see him as he came in here."

"There be no young man, child."

"Lady Grethe, he stood tall, taller than Hals, and did look most sorrowful sad. I saw him."

"Please to ask Rose to come to me, hastily."

Mara ran, affrighted by the sudden strange pallor of Margrethe. When Rose came to the chamber Margrethe said, "Now is my sorrow complete. My son is dead."

"Lady, you cannot know that."

"That was the young man whom you saw enter here."

Rose signed the cross quickly at this.

Margrethe continued, "I felt the warmth of love flooding my heart this morn. The only pictures which came to my mind were of Edward. I did take it to mean that mayhap my father had told him the truth about me, and that Edward would come to visit. He came, but in spirit only."

"How think you he came to die?"

Margrethe sat in silence for a moment. "Helene hath done this. She was root cause of my darkened vision. She killed Ethelred, my husband, although not with her own hand. Now she has destroyed my golden son. What more must I endure? Send me Father John. This will break his old heart and unhinge his mind, I do fear me. He had such love for Edward. Before you go to fetch him, tell me, is my samite gown completed yet?"

"Nay. There be much to do before it be complete."

"Then do naught else. I have much need of that gown. Give the girls holiday from scole. The gown I must have.

And send Hals to take word to Karyl that Edward has been murdered."

Karyl arrived that afternoon. "My lady, I have sent to Torr to inquire if your news be true."

"Hast no faith in my true seeing? Even after the results of my picturings of Padraik's death?"

"Faith, yea, much faith. I did but will this not to be true. We have all done much to preserve the life of the young king."

"I will have need of a white horse."

"There are none white in my stables."

"Then get one. Seldom do I request much of thee, but a white horse I will to have."

"My lady will ride?"

"We will go together for the funeral of my son."

"Is it wise to go to Torr Castle?"

"Helene has cost me my vision, my husband, and now my son. What more could she take save my life? There are times when death be sweeter far than life. I would to be avenged."

"I will send word to King Alfred that Edward is dead as soon as my courier does return from Torr."

"That be good. Should not a guard also be set upon the body of Edward? The one who killed him could also rob him of his funeral if the body do meet with accident."

"I will go myself to set men to keep watch. My men and I will depart for Torr Castle when my courier returns."

"My thanks in all this, Karyl. It is so strange. For William mine eyes did stream with tears. For my own son it is as if the furnace of my hatred has dried up all tears forever. Think you that it would be safe to take Father John with you to Torr? I would that one who loved Edward remain with his body."

"Father John may go with me now. Where be he?"

"In his chamber at his prayers. You know the way?"

"Yea."

"Return soon, Karyl, I have much to plot with you."

✠ ✠ ✠

At Winchester King Alfred sat as one stunned by the impact of the death of his grandson. *Father God and Lord Jesu, your ways are not the ways of men, but why? Why? Why?* So ran his thoughts. *All that I love and cherish is taken from me. Death has devoured my dear wife, my son, my grandson, and Padraik, who was closer than a brother. Sorry misfortune has taken the sight of my daughter. Now I go into old age, too sorrowful to begin another family. I have battled the heathen barbarian and made this into a Christian land, to what end? The kingdom will pass into other hands. Lord of all living, be there reason in all this?*

"Would your majesty that the torches be lighted?"

The question startled King Alfred back to awareness. The room was dim with dusk. A servant stood before him with a kindling torch in his hand.

"Torches? Yea. Eyes want light as heart wants hope. Light them."

His seneschal came, saying, "About tomorrow, your majesty—"

"Let tomorrow decide tomorrow. We go now to the chapel to pray for our dead. If it be that you see the cleric, send him to the chapel."

The hours he spent in the chapel served to quiet his questioning mind. The infirmarian came to the king's chamber as Alfred prepared for bed, bringing him a potion of wine laced with poppy juice. Thanks to the potion, sleep came.

While their king slept, his well-trained servants worked through the night to prepare for the departure from Winchester.

The king's best robes were taken from the privy garde robe and freshened for wearing. Supplies were packed, mounts were curried, weapons polished. All that remained to be done at dawn was for King Alfred to designate who should stay to keep Winchester Castle in order, and who should go to attend the funeral for the young king.

King Alfred's own sarcophagus was placed on a wagon for Edward's use. The lid with the fine effigy of Alfred was removed, and one of plain stone substituted. The new morn was not an hour old when the caravan of sadness set out for Torr Castle.

Rose, at the behest of Margrethe, sent Hals and Tammas together into the forest to bring back luminescent decaying wood. When the two returned they were secretly busy on a project which caused their hands to shine in the darkened room as they ate the evening meal.

Rose herself was busy with the samite gown. This heavy white silk material with gold threads woven into it had been a special gift from Karyl. The material had come from the Orient, at a rare cost.

"Have you cut the sleeves yet?" asked Margrethe.

"Nay, lady, I cuts last what I sews last."

"Then cut them not narrow. I would that they flared out wider from shoulder to wrists, so that the fall of them will be as angels wings."

Tammas came to say that Karyl had brought the white horse. Finding her way with the aid of her walking stick, Margrethe went to the stable.

Karyl asked, "My lady, are you certain that you desire to do this thing?"

"I am."

"Then I will give you all aid possible. Here is the mare. Pure white, as you requested."

Margrethe stroked the soft muzzle and said, "She and I must spend much time together these next few days so that each does know the other well. Who owns her?"

"She belongs to Claud. He has trained her to come to his whistle."

"And is he willing to whistle when I have need?"

"He is."

"Then saddle the white beauty now, and let us ride a way together."

On the day set for Edward's funeral, Margrethe gave Rose leave to take the students and walk up the lane which entered the high road after two leagues. There they could join in with the funeral procession as it passed down the road. Hals and Lisel elected to go with them.

Karyl and two attendant grooms came to escort Margrethe. She sat the white horse, completely veiled in a heavy black veil from head to toe, looking the very model of mourning.

The day had dawned with variable clouds shifting rapidly on the brisk breeze. As they set out for Torr Castle the clouds began to cluster, covering more and more of the sky.

The high road was busy with horsemen and ladies, all being drawn together for the funeral. The main castle gate stood wide. Karyl, Margrethe, and the two grooms rode directly to the stables.

The stables were in an uproar. Strange horses being brought in, which upset the castle horses. Helene's brown mare stood in its stall, fat, well-groomed, and underexercised. Karyl said to his grooms, "You know what to do. Hasten with your task."

The two grooms worked with Helene's horse. One lifted a front hoof, as the other drove an iron spike up through the hoof, almost into the quick. Then they did the same with the other front hoof. The spikes caused no pain at the moment, but they were left deliberately long, so that walking would drive them in deeper. The weight of a rider would hasten the time when the mare would be in pain.

Karyl hid Margrethe away in a rear stall. Covered with the dark veil, none were likely to notice her there. Then Karyl took the two grooms out with him to where the funeral cortege was assembling.

Hundreds were there from the court at Winchester along with the local nobles, ladies, and higher servitors from Torr. Edward's sarcophagus was on a black-draped wagon near the head of the procession. King Alfred was to lead the cortege.

Helene and her ladies came, and their mounts were brought out of the stables for them. Helene rode her mare at a sedate pace, each step driving the sharp iron spikes deeper into the hooves. By the time Helene and her ladies reached their position behind the wagon, the points of the spikes were penetrating into the quick. The mare became restive as the pain shot through her.

Athelstain was locked in his chamber in the King's Tower. Helene considered his grief for Edward unseemly. She would not have him display it in public.

It seemed that now all were assembled. King Alfred began to lead the way from the tournament yard. The heavy wagon creaked to a slow start. Helene nudged her horse. It refused to move. She slapped it with the reins. It still refused to move. Helene gave a yell and hit the mare harder, causing it to whinny and wince, but it refused to walk on its tortured feet.

Suddenly Karyl called out very loudly, "Look! Look there in the stable doorway!"

Margrethe had flung off the mourning veil. In the darkness of the stable doorway she and her horse glowed with an unearthly light as she moved forward, all white and gold, out of the stables. Claud whistled, and the white mare pricked her ears and began to walk slowly in his direction.

At first they all regarded Margrethe as an apparition. Especially as, when she neared the procession, a break in the clouds sent one shaft of sunlight directly down on her. The samite gown glistened and gleamed. Margrethe began to speak in a loud firm voice, raising an arm to point to the direction where Helene must be.

"Behold the murderess! Her horse knows, and will not carry her to the funeral. There sits the one who killed the young king. Hers are the hands which put the poison in his cup."

Helene was taken aback, but managed to say, "Nay, nay. He drowned himself in the well."

"Why lie, Helene, when the eye of heaven witnessed the event? Radnar bore the cup of wine, and you added the poison. You murdered the young king as you murdered his father."

"I did never!"

"Yea. You did. You did not draw the bow, but you made the plot and paid Radnar to do the deed. How does it feel to have killed both father and son?"

Helene said nothing.

"You destroyed a queen."

"I did nothing to the queen."

"You played harlot with the king, besotting him in his bed. How long were you married when your son was born? Weeks only. Yet had effrontery enow to name Ethelred the father."

"Athelstain is his father's child."

"Yea. So be we all," Margrethe turned to face the crowd that she could hear moving restively.

"What say you? Is an adulterous woman to live as queen? Is such to be lauded for destroying the true queen? Is she to be honored for killing her husband? Shall she escape condemnation for the murder of her stepson, our young king?"

King Alfred had halted at the first sound of Margrethe's voice. He turned his horse in time to see a cobble thrown at Helene. Helene tried once more to force her mare to walk, to no avail. The mare stamped her feet, reared up from the pain, and threw Helene off. Margrethe's words had transformed the quiet gentlefolk into a frenzied mob. They surrounded the prostrate Helene, kicking and hitting, avenging themselves for the pain she had caused to others.

Radnar attempted to ride out through the gate, but was quickly captured by Alfred's troops. They led him to the dungeon, where he would keep safe until after the funeral. Helene was not so fortunate. She lay dead and battered beside her mare. King Alfred motioned to the marshals to get the cavalcade started again. They detoured around Helene's body, leaving it for the castle servitors to pick up.

Athelstain strained to see the commotion from his chamber window. He leaned far out, to catch a last glimpse of Edward's sarcophagus. He leaned farther, and lost his balance. He fell from high in the King's Tower onto the tiled roof of the great hall and bounced down into the courtyard. He was dead before he reached the ground.

Margrethe turned toward the castle and raised both arms. "I pronounce a curse upon this place. There will never be joy here again. All who ever dwell here will know deep sorrow. The courtyard gate where Edward was poisoned will admit the traitors who will destroy many kings. The outer walls will stand for a thousand years, but will not protect from death and destruction. Foxes shall den in the great hall, and ravens nest in the towers. Rooks shall cry a dirge over Torr Castle eternally!"

She lowered her arms and called, "Karyl?"

"My lady."

"Karyl, take me home."

"To the scole?"

"Nay. Take me home to your manor. Once I was a princess. Once I was a queen. Once I was a mother. Now I would to be your wife."

The ruins of Torr stand atop their hill to this day. The courtyard gate where Edward was murdered did admit the troops who destroyed all of the inhabitants. The great hall crumbled away, the towers eroded. Birds and beasts make their habitation in the ruins. And over it, in endless spiral flight, the rooks call their dirge.

THE END